EVERY CAT
NEEDS A TOY

April Bonds

authorHOUSE®

AuthorHouse™
1663 Liberty Drive
Bloomington, IN 47403
www.authorhouse.com
Phone: 1 (800) 839-8640

Published by AuthorHouse 02/06/2015

ISBN: 978-1-4969-6921-7 (sc)
ISBN: 978-1-4969-6922-4 (e)

Library of Congress Control Number: 2015902024

Print information available on the last page.

CONTENTS

To my father, who bought me books instead of Barbies, and to my mother, who made me love Laura Ingalls Wilder before kindergarten.

Married more than half a century, you also taught me about love! Robert and Cecelia Johnston, thank you much.

PROLOGUE

My name is Willow, and I live on a commune. Yes, I said a commune. It isn't some weird commune, but it is just a bit odd. Sorry, but I'm very nervous. Soon enough, you will find out why.

I could say that I have no filters, but that really isn't true. I have plenty of filters, but they don't always work when I want them to. Most strangers think I'm rude. I'm not. Just honest. I have a story to tell, and it sounds crazy. I try not to mince words because words are so important in the world I've been raised in. I ask questions constantly, and I put people off. Oh, if you aren't prepared or really confident, I can't warn you about me. Neither can my friends or family. My sisters are appalled by the things I say out loud—sometimes with a foreign accent. I really have to work on my deliveries, and every once in a while, you will need a great Irish bass or a British nanny.

Yes, my parents are those crazy hippies you've heard about who live off the land with like-minded people. I mean, they grow food, play music, make babies, and work hard. It's really a lot of fun, and I am just realizing the lessons I've learned by living this life. I make fun, but it's been a pretty cool existence. We have gardens, animals, flowers, and the sweetest water you have ever tasted. We don't live rough, but we try to live clean. That's a tough thing to do in today's world. Everything seems to be compact and disposable, but what is better than an apple or a pear? Right?

I don't have to go to school, and I still learn amazing things. You might say that my life *is* school, and I have teachers all around me. My dad homeschools me—along with Mom, who prefers artistic things such as speech and cooking. My sisters are much older than me. By the time they married and moved to Texas and Oklahoma, I could barely remember them. I could read and write by the age of three, and I knew every edible and poisonous plant in the area.

My dad is one serious professor. My mom wanted me to learn to control my temper, behave myself, and go to public school. Dad's method won out, and I was homeschooled. Our neighbors have master's degrees in horticulture and engineering. There is no flaking out and no curve in our school system. I spend a lot of time playing outside. I really shouldn't complain when I compare it to public schools. We had plenty of public school kids around us, and I was aware of the program. Of course, parents want the best for their children, but my parents ... Oh, lord. They didn't want me to experience anything outside our own little area.

Our land is in New York—the state, not the city—and it's been in our family for generations. It's an amazing place reserved for people of old, magical powers that are passed down through the generations. The land is magical, and we reap the magic of the ancients. If anyone here knows the origins of this place, they've never told me. I was born in this place, and I assume I will grow old not far from the home I was born in. Time really has no meaning for me. It's all routine. As far as I know, this land has always existed, occupied by people like my parents and their offspring.

Yes, it sounds crazy, but it's true. We are happy people who live with nature the best we can. I've seen the proof of this magic in my parents and our friends and relatives. An orchard that should perish in a drought suddenly blooms with fruit or a field eaten by grasshoppers or worms reaps wheat or corn within a quarter.

We call ourselves the Magicals, and we've finally been able to prove our worth as a society to the New World.

In an amazing election, one of our own won a seat in the New York legislature, and suddenly we are recognized as citizens. We had never had the right to vote. We've lived here for time unknown, but we seem invisible. People can see us, but they can't see us as normal. We aren't immortal or anything, but we don't get sick. Most of our neighbors seem to be middle aged or slightly older, but some are my great-great something or other. There aren't a lot of other kids here, but I'm related to all of them.

It's an amazing thing for the Magicals to finally be recognized as people, but being recognized as citizens of the United States after all the years of isolation was cause for a huge celebration.

CHAPTER 1

The citizenship issue shouldn't have been a thing to celebrate; it was an expected gift, like a wedding present. We had lived here for hundreds of years, taking care of our own without federal help. We'd paid taxes of course. It was something to be expected—not rejoiced—in my opinion.

I was one of the few Magicals who felt this way. The magical people I lived with saw it as a blessing. Many had been here a long, long time, raising crops when others failed. They raised cattle and horses that were the best in milk, meat, toil, and riding. I saw what we provided the world around us. Even in my isolation, I saw things differently. I was naive.

Our elders made their ways through a new society that was completely alien to us. They held jobs, paid taxes, learned the language, and learned the ways of the world. Why shouldn't we be citizens too?

Well, our magic is a sore subject. Yes, we can usually control it, and it isn't always dangerous. The problem is that it can be called by touch, and Americans are so touchy-feely. A handshake here, a man hug there, a pat on the back, even a brush of skin on skin on the subway could make the magic shimmer. Most people can feel it—from simple goose bumps forming from nowhere to electrical shocks. The more magic a person has makes the touch far worse. Most of our magic was bred out of us when Magicals married people outside of our commune, but many citizens had a touch of magic remaining in their blood. If they felt it and fed it, it could grow, but most people were just thinking about getting by.

Most of us are modest with this power, but some have used the magic to further themselves into success as a non-Magical. It isn't a path anyone I know would choose, but rumor says it has happened.

Most of us simply avoid a life that connects us to anyone other than our closest friends and a few nearby communities.

Sensitive strangers might faint or become so entranced when touched by our magic that they will follow us anywhere. Some may orgasm in public. Those are by far the worst to explain.

Imagine someone brushing up against your hand on the subway, and suddenly he's convulsing and screaming your name in orgasmic joy! Yeah, it's a sight to behold—and one you don't want to experience more than once.

Basically, we avoid most physical contact. Obviously, this was almost impossible since we lived in rural New York. Trips to the city were frequent, and the bumping and jarring of millions of people among us was inevitable. I hated the trips to the city. No one even noticed me unless they brushed up against my skin and the magic prickled. I was simple and average to the big-city people. Only a few would stare at me without touching and think I was special or different. Most of my experiences happened before I found out I was cursed. I never could have imagined what would become of me in those last few months while I lived comfortably and happily with my parents. It was lovelier after my two older sisters got married and moved away.

It could be the result of my curse. So many distractions. Ah, the distractions. Yes, I'm cursed. I was free until July. I was born free from any curse, but as I grew into a woman, Aphrodite took an interest in me out of boredom. Now I am destined to never find a suitable husband or anyone who will love me completely.

Aphrodite cursed me for startling her son. Thanks, Mom-in-Law!

The summer of my eighteenth year and of the celebration, I was brought to Aphrodite's attention. I had no idea what had become of me that summer in the shadows of the Catskills. We had few mirrors, and all my baggy hand-me-down clothes still fit. I was trying to decide on a dress to wear to the celebration, but nothing seemed to fit. My chest was too large, my waist too narrow, and my hips were too wide. In exasperation, I went to my mother. She was a willowy blond with long limbs and few curves—it was as if her name should be Willow instead of mine. Her name is Brenda, but she's often called Bren.

She looked at me and said, "We must go shopping."

I'd never heard those words from my mother's mouth. She hated the city as much, if not more, than I did. We went shopping anyway.

It was a beautiful early summer day. The blue sky and slight breeze made everything possible. My mother rented a car so we didn't have to interact with anyone else. We rarely did things like this. We normally took public transportation and taxis, but whenever the need arose, the money for luxury was there. Touching on public transportation was always an issue. Bren's beauty made it even more awful.

I watched the sights through the tinted windows. All the people and hurried activity amazed me. We worked hard on the commune, but we weren't stressed or urgent people. All I could feel was stress and urgency; it looked exhausting to me! My mother acted as if this was a regular occurrence—as if she belonged to this life of indulgence even though I had seen her go without. Many times, our family and neighbors where the best off because of my parents' attention.

She gazed forward, focused on the clock. She looked and acted like the princess I had always believed she was. I was astounded by her poise and decorum.

Brenda was a giver not a spender, and the trip seemed like a dream. I wondered exactly who this woman beside me was as she turned and smiled at me. I loved her with all my heart.

I had never questioned why or how we had ended up at the commune or how we earned money. The money was always there, somehow, from somewhere. It was a life I loved and believed in. My parents were the best!

We shopped for hours in vintage boutiques and upscale stores. I tried on beautiful dresses, one after another. The salespeople in the stores were awed by how all the clothes looked so gorgeous! I was ecstatic! It was more fun than I'd ever imagined, and Bren and I laughed and hugged. We had lunch on the private balcony of a fellow Magical's condo (a new word for me), and it was delicious. We ate salads with greens and reds so deep they stung our eyes, chicken salad that was to die for, and crème brûlée for desert. It satisfied our shopping starvation. We devoured every morsel. Shopping was hard work.

We purchased a whole new wardrobe, including bras, underwear, socks, and shoes. My mom was a great shopper. She saw things I'd simply pass by as too beautiful or flattering. It seemed as if money were no object and we spent hours on shoes alone! I found it hilarious since we wore two pair of boots at home, waterproof and not. She had flair and taste—even if it was rarely seen in our normal lives.

For some reason, she went for flattering and flirtatious. I saw something in my mother that day that spoke of younger, more salacious times. Brenda chose clothing that accented my chest and my curves. She held various colors up to my pale skin to find the most flattering shades with my straight blond hair. She bought me pants that left no curve to the imagination, shirts with lots of cleavage, and dresses that swirled around my newfound body. I couldn't really object because she was right—they looked great! We picked out jewelry that was striking but not overwhelming, shoes I could actually walk in, and purses with tiny pockets to store whatever I needed. We purchased makeup and perfume, which I had never worn. I was shocked and pleased with my new self. Plus, she was paying with some unknown fund I never imagined existed.

I wore a white knee-length cotton dress with lots of floral embroidery to the celebration. It was strapless, but I felt comfortable in it. Purple violets and green leaves trailed down one side and around the hem. I wore a low silver-heeled sandal and a silver bracelet with green stones that matched my earrings. I had taken off the only necklace I'd ever worn, a small arrow pendent in gold and encircled by a heart of pink gems. I had no idea where it came from, but I had always had it. I felt a little naked without it, but I also felt beautiful, flirty, and attractive. I was certain my mother would have chosen one of the sexier dresses. I didn't mind. All the things my mother thought might entice a man or boy were not my style, but the dress made me feel like the adult I was becoming.

Unfortunately, it also brought me to Aphrodite's notice. Violets are Psyche's flower from Eros or Cupid—depending on the country—and the green stone symbolized fertility. If I had known, I would have worn the red chiffon, but who knows what that would have caused? I hadn't realized my connection yet with ancient history, and I had a great time laughing, dancing, eating, and flirting. Boys I had known my entire life were begging to be my next dance partner, to bring me a drink or snack, or just shuffling around me.

The goddess of love felt my presence and joy for life, and she fumed! She recognized my reincarnated spirit, and she had always hated Psyche. Maybe she didn't like all the attention I received—or maybe she liked it too much. She was a very jealous and arrogant woman. I can say that since I really don't give a damn anymore. She's tried to ruin my life so many times that I hate her just as much as she hates me.

My evening went on more beautifully than I could have prayed for at the time. It seemed like a dream. If I could have imagined what danger I was in, I could have prepared myself a little better.

However, a woman of eighteen is really no more than the child she was just a few months ago. I understood dating and sex since there were so few secrets in our community—or so I thought.

CHAPTER 2

I danced with a lot of boys from outside the commune that night, mostly neighbors. Flirting inside the commune stunk way too much of incest—even if we weren't related. I'd known these boys for far too long to think of them as more than brothers. Even though some had grown into gorgeous men, I still saw them as friends.

There were some other boys from the community and other similar communes. When my sisters married, they moved away to other homes of the Magicals. One went to Texas, and the other went to Oklahoma. With their boring husbands and mean attitudes, I wasn't sorry they were so far away. It made my life a lot easier.

Many of the boys were familiar with our way of life, which made them far more attractive than boys out in the real world. It's really hard to explain our lifestyle to someone who has never lived it.

I danced and drank strawberry wine for the first time. I was treated as a woman instead of the child I had been just yesterday. I felt strong and beautiful and peaceful.

I danced with my father with his strange East Indian clothes and his goofy moves. Obren is amazing in his own way. He loves life more than anyone I have ever met, and he loves my mother and sisters above all others—just as we love him. He's exuberant and friendly and tells the silliest jokes. He can talk to anyone about anything, and he's also never met a stranger. His salt-and-pepper hair was braided almost to his waist, and he never stopped smiling during the entire dance.

The area was set with beautiful flowers and fully grown trees. Hibiscus, honeysuckle, and willows could be seen from every angle. Homegrown fruits and vegetables overflowed every table. A goat and a pig were roasting on spits. The smell in the air was delicious and tantalizing. It overcame everything in the nearby area, and it seemed to attract even more boys and every man from the area. I was never alone or without food or a drink in my hand. Never had I felt more beautiful.

Little did I know that the attention I received that evening was more than Aphrodite could stand. As I've said before, she was a jealous and petty goddess. Who was I to compete with the goddess of love? No one. I had never been beautiful or flirtatious. I had never been popular or particularly funny to anyone but my dad or me. I couldn't even grasp what was happening. But in me, she saw Psyche drawing everyone's attention away from her. For no reason I could fathom, every single man in the group seemed to flock to little old me! It was enticing and exciting and really undeserved, I felt. Who was I but another pretty face?

I was obviously more than just a pretty face to Aphrodite. No one had ever challenged Aphrodite in her beauty or would even dare—except for Psyche in a lifetime I knew nothing about.

People had stopped worshiping at the temples of Aphrodite. They had stopped pleading her to help them find true love. Worst of all, they no longer recognized her as the goddess of beauty. She was so angry, insulted, desolate, and dejected—all because of me. She wanted me to be her surrogate in sex, her portal to this world, as if a sort of conduit. She wanted to use me to satisfy her loneliness and ignite the human need for her special qualities. Is this what she would ask of me to ensure that I follow through? At the time, it was all a mystery to me. Although, thinking back, I could feel something brewing. Something I had no control over.

How could she possibly choose an innocent such as me? It could mean having sex with several of the other living gods, goddesses, demigods and even the lesser gods if she required it. A virgin, a plain simple girl from a commune, a competitor of the Greek goddess of love? She has lost her mind!

I'd asked for none of this, and I craved none of this.

That was Aphrodite's desire, not mine.

CHAPTER 3

Boys really never paid any attention to me. Really. My friends and cousins had boys flocking around them, but I never did. I was simply Willow, no one special. I was newly clothed and suddenly curvy, and I'd always been petite.

Boys treated me as a sister or good friend, and that was always okay. I was the girl they taught to juggle or pulled weeds with. I was as likely to push them in the creek as they were. And I didn't squeal—ever. But tonight was different.

I had had a small crush on a boy from my previous school. I had kissed Kevin in the lunchroom under the table in kindergarten. He hadn't paid attention to me since. I knew it was a stupid crush, but who forgets their first kiss? Even if it is on the cheek? His dark, wavy hair, deep blue eyes, and single dimple in his left cheek made him cake for my eyes. His perfect white smile was a prize to behold. I must admit I was mesmerized!

He was dressed in perfect jeans—fitted and worn—with a white tailored T-shirt with a black skull on the front and the words, "To live or die?" as a question on the back. He looked scrumptious. Black motorcycle boots and a studded belt completed his bad boy outfit. I didn't think he really was a bad boy, but the look definitely suited him. Several other girls noticed as well.

Kevin asked me to dance, and we danced. I was delighted. After a fast song, the lights turned down. A slow song began, and electricity licked the air around us. He smiled, pulled me closer, and wrapped his arm around my waist. I could feel a pull deep within me that I couldn't explain. I was a little breathless from the fast dance, and I found myself unable to breathe. It felt so perfect and so different. I was afraid to inhale his scent. *Please don't let me hyperventilate! What is this I'm feeling?* I felt as if I'd separated from myself. He pressed his chest to mine, a mighty fine chest, and we began to sway to the music.

I felt myself being pulled in by his heart pulsing against mine, pulled by his presence, his energy—and I'm sorry to say now—his fascination with me! Me!

I was fascinated that he was fascinated. I leaned in slightly to smell his scent. He smelled of cologne and youth and sunshine. It was summer after all.

I suppose he felt it as an invitation because he hesitantly leaned in toward me and took in my scent.

"You smell of springtime and ... and ... jasmine?" he said as if he had read my mind. His smile entranced me. He hesitated, a pause I didn't understand, and then he leaned down and kissed me softly on the lips. It was so soft and gentle, almost a whisper before it deepened. It was an exquisite kiss. Soft and lingering, but bold and attentive. It was everything I'd dreamed of since I was five years old under the lunch table.

We danced all evening together only stopping for a sip of wine or a snack. Other boys tried to break in the dance, but Kevin said no to all of them—and not always politely.

The last dance of the night arrived all too soon. It was a slow samba with lots of hip movements and very close contact. It was a very encouraging last dance. He held my body close as we swayed to the Latin beat. His steps and guidance were perfect.

I was glad I'd been forced to go to cotillion, a dance and manners class for adolescents that is sure to scar a person for life. I had learned to samba and put every ounce of energy into it—and so did Kevin. Our bodies swayed and dipped and glided, and I felt drunk with the music. At the end of the dance, I was breathless. He gallantly dipped me and gently kissed my … forehead?

My forehead? After all that? Seriously? What is up with this dude?

An unrecognized frustration tore through my mind. Aphrodite was angry.

CHAPTER 4

I went home. Our house was a modern cabin. Meaning, it had electricity and heating, but we didn't have air-conditioning. Normally, we didn't need it, but that night it seemed as though we did. It seemed unusually hot after that samba! *Ugh!* I blew my hair out of my face, and my shoulders drooped in disappointment.

Electricity played in the air as if a storm were coming. It tingled up my skin, and my hair clung to my face.

I slipped out of my white party dress, slipped on a nightgown, and went down the hall to wash my face and brush my teeth. As I finished, I felt a flush up against my leg. It felt like the heater was on. I looked down, but nothing was there. Why was I so warm? I fanned myself and realized that I would need the fan on. I went to my bed and crawled under my sheets and my new quilt.

I thought about Kevin. I couldn't help myself.

My great grandmother had made the quilt, a starburst pattern of blue and green with roses and lavender scraps. I didn't remember her at all, but the quilt was a tradition. It is given to a girl when she reached adulthood so she could find a perfect, magical mate. Magical because we are Magicals. At the time, I didn't understood how magical I was. I had no idea what power I possessed—or even if I had any at all. I would not know for a long, long time.

Bren had spread the quilt across the bed while I got ready for the party. I stopped short the second I saw it, but it was beautiful.

I felt guilty sleeping under it for the first time since the only attraction I'd had for a man was Kevin. And he was so not magical.

I needed a fan, but I was too exhausted to hunt one down and plug it in. It was going to be a long night. Finally, I fell into a fitful sleep after tossing and turning. It was so unlike my normal easy sleep that I finally just sat up on the side of the bed with my chin resting on my hand. I looked toward my only window at the same time that pebbles rained down upon it. I let out a silly squeak as I reached for the curtains. I hated myself for that squeak.

Kevin was standing at the window with a handful of pebbles.

He waved me down with a few flickering fingers and a huge smile. I knew I'd never let him in my room. But how could I resist going down to him?

I silently dressed in cutoff warm-ups and a T-shirt, my normal comfy attire. My face was cleaned of makeup, and my straight hair was lank and damp. I quickly pulled it into my normal ponytail. I couldn't imagine that I looked the least bit attractive, but I needed to hear what Kevin had to say about this evening—about kissing me so passionately and then finishing with the kiss on the forehead after the sexiest moment I had ever imagined during the samba.

I walked softly through the hallway, knowing every creak of the hardwood, and out the front door that my father kept heavily oiled so it wouldn't squeak. It wasn't the first time I had snuck out, but the first time for this reason. I wish I had been more awake, less giddy, more in tune with the world, but I only had questions on my mind.

Without a noise, I walked out of my family home and into a goddess's curse and Kevin's arms.

CHAPTER 5

In the moonlight, Kevin looked gorgeous in his jeans and T-shirt. His muscled arms and chest were so perfect in the night air. He had one hand in his pocket, and the other hand held four perfect white rosebuds.

The flowers promised what could come, a beautiful flower waiting to bud. It felt as if he knew me better than anyone ever had. He lifted his fingers to call me out of the house, and I smiled. He held out the roses and offered a gorgeous smile that lit up his eyes and tickled things deep within me. When I reached him, he drew me into a deep hug and rocked me back and forth like a child. He gently kissed me on each eyelid and each cheek and smiled. "Do you like the flowers?"

I could only nod. I took the flowers from him, and every feeling that flooded me showed on my face. I was certain he could see straight through me. I'd never felt anything like it. *Is this what love feels like? Maybe the wine has gone to my head.*

He kissed me heartily, and I kissed him back with as much passion. I just couldn't help myself. My body ached and burned to be near him. We kissed under the moonlight in my front yard, and our hands explored each other's backs, arms, and necks. My hands seemed to gravitate toward his dark, wavy hair. It melted in my hands like chocolate, and I could barely move.

When he offered me his hand to lead me to his car, I felt hesitant. I needed some time alone with him to explore these strange new feelings. I felt alive for the first time in my life. I felt wanted. I felt awakened. I wanted to talk to him, get to know him better, and kiss some more.

As we scooted into the backseat for comfort, I smelled ivy and roses. The roses seemed obvious from the rosebuds, but the scent was so much stronger. The ivy was strong and pungent. I wondered what Kevin had left in his car to rot, and then I pushed the thought away.

Kevin gave me a look I didn't recognize. He pushed his lips against mine painfully, and he fell on top of me, kissing me far too roughly. Holding my wrists in his hands, his body pressed to mine. My mouth was heartily covered by his. *I don't know what to do. Do I like him? I just want him to stop. I want him to talk to me. This is not right! This is too far, too fast.* I wanted him off of me more than anything. I had thought we could talk and get to know each other better. He had a different idea of getting to know me.

I pushed him back, but it was futile. He was much stronger than I was. He was much too big for me to push away. He abused my mouth until it felt bruised, and then he began pulling my clothes off. I tried desperately to fight and scream, but he covered my mouth with his. I knew that my body was not my own. Tears ran down my checks and pooled in my ears as I begged him to stop. My muffled words meant nothing to him. I felt him grind his pelvis into mine, causing it to bruise and ache. He held me so tightly with his strong hands that I could barely move. I could barely breathe.

He ripped my shirt from my body and sunk his head between my breasts. I screamed, but he put his hand over my mouth as he kissed and bit my breasts. I had never known such fear or such "love." *What the hell is this? I have no idea!* It was the attention I had wanted—yet it was unwanted now. I was terrified! This was not love or even lust. This was abuse.

He took my bra and shoved it into my mouth while I was trying to scream for help. He pulled my shorts and panties down and shoved himself into me. I felt my body tear apart and smelled the metallic scent of blood as I struggled fruitlessly. It was a painful and humiliating shock. I froze in that moment.

He may have been surprised for a moment by my body's resistance, but he never stopped or slowed down. I screamed my pain into the gag in my mouth. It was a painful initiation into the adult world. I was rocked with it, and I cried out, but I think it excited him more. He pushed in and out as I sobbed into my bra. *God, it hurts. Please stop. Please die now.* I tried to cry out, to tell him to stop, but I could barely breathe. He forced his way into my unwilling body four or five times, which seemed like a thousand. I screamed into my bra gag and his hand, and then he shuddered against me. I was trembling, freezing, and sweating at the same time. Haze filled my eyes, and I knew the feeling of shock.

He lay on top of me silent, still. God, I hoped he was dead. He looked up at me with shining eyes and smiling teeth that were so straight and white. "Thank you! That was great!" he said with a smirk.

I was completely numb. I couldn't think or say a word.

He said something, but I couldn't understand or comprehend the words.

I gathered what was left of my clothes, and sobbing for my pain and shame, I entered my house as silently as I had left it. The same house I had left less than an hour before. However, I would never be the same again.

I threw my clothes away in a neighbor's trashcan, took a two-hour shower, and went to bed.

I hated myself.

CHAPTER 6

You come to me at night.
I feel your presence,
You hold me tight.
We talk,
All innocent,
We never touch,
I love you.

I cried myself to sleep that night. I sobbed until I hiccupped—and then I sobbed some more without relief. I couldn't believe what had happened to me. Of all the girls I knew, no one ever spoke of such pain and embarrassment. I had trusted him. I couldn't imagine another boy I'd grown up with treating a woman in such a way. *He is an animal!*

I fell into a restless, crying sleep and let my sadness overwhelm me. I hurt. I needed a long soak in a bath, and the shower hadn't cut it, but I was far too sore to move. I was broken, but I yearned for someone to love me—to really and truly love me. Kevin acted as if he cared for me, but he had broken me and hurt me. I had prayed for a deep, insatiable love, but I didn't dream it existed. I didn't believe it could ever be real. My parents were the only exception, and I could imagine my mother clawing my father's eyes out while he slept if he ever treated her in such a way. I wished I could claw Kevin's eyes out.

In my dreamless, semisleep, I felt the bed bow next to me. It was as if someone had sat down on the opposite side. I froze. I slowed my breath and pulse as if I was sleeping peacefully. I thought it was Kevin coming back for more, and I jerked to my side to see who was there.

The stranger next to me was beautiful, and he had dark hair and deep, green eyes. He carried a bow and arrow that was pointed at my hip. I flipped over, and his bow went south. The arrow nicked his thigh. He stared at his leg as the blood dripped. I tried to scream, but his gaze silenced me. I couldn't make a single sound except the rush of air entering and leaving my frightened lungs.

As he raised his eyes to mine, lightning flashed outside. It seemed to move through his irises, and his green eyes electrified. He studied me with an unwavering gaze. It was as if he had never seen a woman before. "I'm so sorry!" he said.

His delicate hand reached out to brush the tearstains on my cheeks. He slowly and deliberately lifted his fingers to his mouth to kiss away the tears. He smiled a gorgeous smile at me and proclaimed, "No one shall ever hurt you again, Willow, goddess, be my witness."

I couldn't imagine why he knew my name. Nothing mattered anymore.

The thunder outside cracked loudly, and the lightning felt like it was in the room instead of miles away. It cracked so loudly that I jumped and grabbed his hand. I looked down at our joined hands and felt a stirring in my heart. I saw the same light in his eyes as he lifted my hand to his lips.

I was stupefied by all that had happened and the stranger in front of me.

He gently kissed my hand without ever losing eye contact. "My name is Eros, and I have been sent for you—and you alone."

"Why are you sorry?" I asked.

"Because my mother will never forget this, my love."

CHAPTER 7

"How could you?" Aphrodite screamed loudly enough to shake the stones of her temple. "I gave you one simple task—to remove this small, mortal, girl child from my life—and you did this? Eros, my child, don't you know your own responsibilities? Do you know what you have done to us? This is Psyche all over again! I will not, will not, will not be replaced again! Do you understand, Eros?"

Eros bowed his head in defeat. *Must I go through this again?* "I'm sorry, Mother! She's so innocent and beautiful!"

"More beautiful than me?" she growled.

Eros paused, thinking of the nick on his thigh from his love-struck arrow. "Of course not, Mother. You shouldn't concern yourself." Eros looked down and thought of his beloved and the pain she had suffered.

Aphrodite realized her dilemma and decided to take control.

I feel as if I'm visibly altered, but no one seems to notice the difference in me. My parents still see me as their same daughter; my few friends laugh and joke with me. But I am different, altered.

Perhaps, I am broken. I am not the same. I have been raped, and I have lost all my hopes and dreams for a husband and family. Kevin has taken it all from me. Even if Eros meant to give it all back, I still felt that I was walking in a minefield of unrequited desire. And what did his mother have to do with it? He's a grown man. Why would she care? He obviously knew what had happened that night. Did he see it and not stop it? Why me?

Eros filled my mind. I feel violated, strangely absorbed. I can't get him out of my mind, my every movement. Was he Cupid with his love spells? He said his name was Eros. I looked it up on Google. Guess what? One and the same, and he'd misfired, so to say. What did that mean?

My life seems to no longer be my own. Eros, whoever he is, holds my future dreams in his hands. I have no control over my feelings. Vacillating between sadness and remorse, I tried to walking through my daily life, feeding the sheep and pigs, and tilling the garden. Nothing looked the same around me, but everything seemed to be larger than life, more focused, more enhanced.

Eros appears in my dreams—but not in my life. He loves me and offers me platitudes and poetry. He feels my pain and suffers it with me. He gently soothes my broken soul, dream word by dream word. He offers himself to me. Somehow he takes most of the pain away, psychologically and emotionally.

His offer is an offer no one in my situation could accept. When that doesn't help, he offers me his protection.

Protection sounds like something I could use, but I'm not sure. I'm scared. Scared is something I'm completely unused to.

My home and community were places of peace and happiness. Kevin tried a couple of times to find me, and I told my parents he wasn't my type. They covered for me graciously, and Kevin just as graciously tried his best to charm them into seeing me. Luckily, they trusted me more than him.

Eros arrives again and again, at night, in my dreams. He becomes my hero, my lord, my king, but he never manifests himself in human form. I wonder who and what is holding him back? He obviously loves me, but he is distant and unreachable. Where does he come from? How does he enter my mind in such a lazy fashion?

Little did I know he was a god—and I will always be his goddess. Aphrodite would never accept our union.

Eros, who are you? Why me? I ask this question several times a day, but no answer comes. *I feel as if I don't exist. How did this happen?*

It happened because his mother is jealous of me. Aphrodite expected him to shoot his loving arrow into my hip and force me to fall in love with an awful being, such as Kevin or anyone else of her choosing. She had no idea that I would startle him and cause him to shoot the arrow into his own leg, making him my servant in love and passion for eternity. *That's an awfully long time!*

She doesn't agree with the situation, and Eros refuses to shoot his arrows anymore.

Men and animals stop reproducing all over the earth. The world is in turmoil. No children or animals are conceived, and Aphrodite is desolate. Without love and consummation, she will lose all her powers. I can only imagine what it is like to be powerful—and then having no power at all.

Aphrodite was angry and basically ravenous since love and desire are her food. In a desperate attempt to change things, she promises Eros that if he will shoot his arrows, he can have me when the time is right.

She never mentioned the conditions of when that time might be or her hatred for when she made the agreement.

Eros agreed.

Chapter 8

I shoot my arrow of love.

It strikes flesh.

The medicine seeps in.

It courses through my veins.

This feeling I have,

My love for you.

Eros began shooting his arrows again, and life returned to normal. Except for me, life would never normal again.

Animals and humans reproduced, but life was not as it once was. Spouses argued. Children disappeared in the wilderness. Crops were eaten by grazers, but no grazers were found to be hunted. Meat eaters were much harder to find and hunt. The rains stopped, and the crops failed in the fields. Even fertile couples with several children lacked the ability to reproduce. The Magicals no longer had power over the land or the crops, and the weak and elderly were slowly dying. Life was hard.

We simply stagnated. Our commune was in despair. We had never experienced a famine or drought that a touch of a finger or a lilting melody couldn't resolve. All the Magicals worked the normal wonders to no avail. Finally, the understanding for us all began to sink in. We knew we would starve by winter because our stores would be depleted.

I felt the goddess calling to me. Aphrodite and Eros urged me toward something. I had no idea what it was. I began to tremble and grew cold or unusually warm from time to time. My hands trembled all the time.

She had my number, but I had no idea what she wanted or who she was. I craved the love of Eros, a love his mother would never allow me to act upon. She put other men in my way. She tried to distract me so I could feed her needs. She let my feelings of desire once more—for Eros and for life and love in general.

Boys from my community began to visit my house regardless of my trembling hands. They were generally nice boys who seemed interested in me, but they were mostly boring. Some of these boys— or men—I'd known my entire life. They flattered and enticed me and tried to make me laugh or smile during those dire times, but I simply couldn't pretend.

After a month, one particular boy finally caught my eye. Flyn was a year older than me. He was cute, soft spoken, and gentle. He loved music and laughing. As he spoke to me, he looked in my eyes and seemed to anticipate what I might say. It was as if he really wanted to know what I was thinking. It stunned me! He actually listened to me. Our friendship became an obsession. I dreamed about him and wished he would pull me close and hold me. We laughed a lot and shared our thoughts and emotions. We listened to music and argued about lyrics.

We stretched out on the couch and watched movies or sports and talked. Flyn really wanted to talk to me. We talked about our hopes, dreams, and regrets. He would touch me sweetly on the knee or shoulder and tell me that everything would be okay. He was the first person I told about Kevin, and he held me so softly and whispered in my ear that I wasn't to blame.

As our friendship blossomed rapidly, reality hit me. We talked about old times and laughed. Flyn's fingers held mine softly and gently. He felt good and comfortable, and I knew Flyn wanted me for who I was. He ran his hand through my hair, and he loved the fragrance of it. I could see it in his eyes. That much was clear, but was I ready to give up on Eros? What if he was as evil as Kevin? I didn't believe he could be. He was my dear, sweet friend.

Flyn had a gorgeous smile, and his dimples lit up his beautiful, brown eyes. His body was perfectly sculpted, and he had curly hair. He spoke softly and kindly and held my hand as if it were a jewel. He had the softest hands I had ever felt, and I imagined what they would feel like against my skin. *I definitely have to make the effort to use more lotion.* What was going to happen was inevitable. We both felt it in our bones.

My only experience had involved pain, but Flyn offered protection and love. He offered acceptance, and he offered his heart. He was the prize!

I knew my hand was no jewel, but the way he looked at me made my insides melt.

The first time he kissed me, he kept his eyes open and watched my response. He was tentative yet courageous. He had no idea how I would react. He was exactly the man I needed to heal my pain. I was momentarily stunned, and then I felt a surge of energy in my stomach. It was what I was aching for! Our tongues tangled together, and the softest lips I'd ever felt became one with mine. He was my savior from all I had suffered at the hands of Kevin, Aphrodite, and Eros.

A week later, we made love by the lake. Since I was no longer a virgin, thanks to Kevin, it was smooth and playful. We enjoyed each other's bodies as they were meant to be enjoyed. As he slipped off my clothes, I became shy, but once his lips touched mine, my hands were all over him. I removed his clothing and rejoiced in his chiseled muscles. We enjoyed it again, slower. He explored my body, kissed my neck and shoulders, and nibbled my collarbones, which sent chills to the center of my core. He paid each breast and nipple loving attention—kissing, sucking, and nibbling. His hands searched ever lower to my abs, tense with desire, and lower between my legs to that spot still wet with his release. He teased and taunted me, making me spasm again and again until he plunged into me to his depth and took his energy out on me. I was boneless.

It was everything I had ever imagined it would be. Flyn held me and kissed me as if I was the most precious of beings. He told me how long he had waited for someone like me and how much he loved me. I loved him back without ever thinking and with all my heart.

I was cursed. Aphrodite had ensured that I would never find true love or a soul mate. I hoped Flyn was that man, but I would never know for sure.

Flyn and I immediately moved to a small trailer in the commune. No one expected us to make special vows or promises, but our happiness was enough to please our friends and family. For three beautiful spring months, we shared a life. We worked together, played together, and made love frequently—very, very frequently.

As Flyn and I progressed in our relationship, odd things seemed to arise. We had typical things that occurred in any relationship: space issues and concerns over money and past relationships. Even though we were blissfully happy in the beginning, it just couldn't last. I see that now.

Arguments became our choice of communication. He didn't understand me. How could I ever trust him to be my one and only?

He had women chasing after him everywhere we went, and my heart broke every time. I knew it was jealousy and insecurity on my part. Simply because he had a normal life before me shouldn't have hurt things. I just couldn't stand the competition, and he couldn't stand my withdrawal.

I felt myself withdrawing from the relationship, but I was helpless to stop it.

Aphrodite loved it and fed on the jealousy and pettiness. Of course, she was behind it all.

Flyn was everything a mortal man could possibly be for her. She even fed on the make-up sex, which was always amazing. Always focusing on my pleasure, Flyn was the perfect lover. He taught me to feel again. But how could Flyn continue to compete with Eros and my connection with Aphrodite and Psyche?

It was always there, like a deep, dark cloud over our heads.

I can't blame him. It was an incredible connection that I couldn't explain.

After days and weeks of fighting, making up, crying, and cuddling, we just couldn't do it anymore. We were emotionally spent and cried our good-byes to each other. We separated with a fingertip through a car door window, tears flowing. We went our separate ways, knowing we loved each other. Sometimes love isn't enough.

CHAPTER 9

I call for you.
Never appears.
Felt your wind upon me,
Your lips touch my neck,
I turn around.
It was just the wind,
Never to be.

"How could you dare let that one get past you? Stupid, stupid son! She cared for him and he for her! What were you thinking?" Aphrodite screamed at Eros, shattering glass and windows around her temple.

Nymphs and Naiads scattered haphazardly around the potted plants and water gardens tended by them. The rise of her hatred grew louder and louder until it sounded like thunder on earth.

Eros simply bowed his head and muttered a soft apology, but he meant none of it. Flyn was not right for his sweet Willow. He could never explain that to his mother. He couldn't tell her how he could never give up his love for a human girl or how the fire of his arrow burned in his soul. He'd be damned if he ever released Willow from the spell that bound them, a spell of his mother's making, but a spell even she could never break.

Willow would know only one true love, his own. He knew he could keep that promise, and no mortal man would ever touch her again.

"Who does she think she is?" Aphrodite yelled to Athena.

"Perhaps a girl in love? You did send Eros after her, didn't you? Isn't that the job you gave him? Madam?"

Aphrodite cast lightning eyes at Athena over the use of a word that meant "old woman" in her mind. She murmured and moved toward the center of her temple clearly agitated. "If she thinks she can claim my only son again, she has no idea who she is dealing with!" Aphrodite pounded her hand on a column.

Athena leaned back on the soft cushions, smiled at Aphrodite, and said, "Why fight it?"

Aphrodite laughed beneath her breath. Athena loved a good fight. She demurely covered a wicked grin with a perfectly gorgeous hand. "Yes, dear. She has no idea who she is dealing with. Absolutely none."

CHAPTER 10

When I left Flyn that day, I was a broken woman. I was hurt, and I knew I had hurt him. It wasn't in my nature to hurt another being, especially one I loved. I couldn't have prepared myself better for what was to come. Flyn did love me, and except for this crazy universe that I didn't understand—and the processes of life—I could have been happy with him. But I was cursed. Cursed! And no matter how perfect we seemed to be, I couldn't stay. I was forced to move, to proceed with my unknown future. I turned my back on what could have been a happy and peaceful life because I had no choice in the matter.

The blue sky looked sad and gray to me, even though it had white, wispy clouds scattered about. It had rained hard earlier, and I felt more like that was what I deserved. However, I had no say in what my heart told me. I was meant to be the wife of a god. I was undoubtedly in love with Eros, though I had only once seen his face, and that may have been one of my nightly dreams of him.

I couldn't return to my parents' house while they were home. Not with the guilt I felt. I waited until they were both gone and collected a few things that I had left there. I drove off into the midday sun toward my closest sister's house in Texas. I felt that Rose would surely welcome me since she and her husband didn't have children yet. I hoped she would give me advice about my love life. She was ten years older than me, and we didn't have much of a relationship, but I grabbed the birthday card she had sent me, a backpack of food and water, a few tools, and a suitcase of my favorite clothes. I left a note for my parents and turned my car south toward Fort Worth.

My radio sucked and sporadically picked up a channel. I had a tape player and some songs I had recorded over the years, but I preferred the silence. I had a lot to think about, and my tears followed me on the road. I was crying for my parents, for Flyn, for Eros, and for myself. I dried my tears with my sleeve and was glad I'd left all that makeup behind with Bren.

I'd really never driven long distances alone, and I stopped and bought a map, more snacks, and more gas. It would be a long trip, and I had no idea what to expect when I arrived. I assumed my parents would find my note and call Rose to alert her before I arrived.

I had only seen my sisters for brief periods during the summer or winter solstices since I was three. I had no idea what to expect when I arrived at Rose's house, but I couldn't have anticipated my unwelcome.

CHAPTER 11

Eros wandered his mother's home and temple but avoided contact with her as much as possible. She knew him too well to expect him to spend much time with her. She knew his mind was on Willow anyway. She was so like Psyche, and it was painful to remember the loss of her. Born a mortal but loved by him, Psyche had become a demigod. She bore a daughter (Pleasure), but after a few thousand years, Psyche died a peaceful death in the arms of her husband, Cupid. She learned that love was the most dangerous of all emotions for a human or a god.

Eros changed his name and withdrew inside himself. Eros was disturbed by the memories and aching for his lost love (Psyche) and their daughter (Pleasure). He mumbled to himself as he walked Aphrodite's gardens. Pleasure had cast herself down into the human world soon after Psyche left the godly world for the afterlife, and she was quite busy. She found great joy in her manipulations on earth. Eros hadn't seen Pleasure in eons, but he saw her havoc in the earthly realm. Pleasure had so many qualities of his mother that he wondered how she was the child of his marriage to the sweet and diligent Psyche. His daughter was a complete mystery to him, but his mind and dreams where wrapped up in Willow. His link with her through the power of his fiery arrows allowed him to visit her on a subconscious level. Once she allowed her mind to be unshielded, he could go to her, hold her, love her, and caress her. Through her eyes, he could see a kaleidoscope of life, like the scrolls his Aunt Athena held so tightly.

To Eros, it was real and almost satisfying, but Willow only remembered it as a dream. He gazed into her blue eyes and ran his hands over her smooth blond hair. He wished she would know that he was with her and not simply a dream she barely remembered in the morning. If only she knew he was there for her—even if he couldn't be present in her waking life.

Damn my mother to rot in the river Styx for the rest of her days! he thought.

He had to be very careful to contain these thoughts. Many of her servants knew him well and could read his emotions, having been gifted the power from Aphrodite. Once again, his mother used others with her powers of persuasion. She could be so charming, but he somehow loved her. Everyone loved her; she was Aphrodite, after all. She was manipulative and selfish, and Eros was lonely. He'd been alone for far too long, and though no one could ever replace the love he had shared with Psyche, Willow was the first and only woman to entice him. He recognized that he had accidentally shot himself with his own fiery arrow of love, but it never would have happened if she hadn't been so strikingly beautiful as she rolled over and turned her fearful, beautiful, broken eyes toward him. He only wanted to comfort her in that moment.

Usually he was good at his job and wasn't distracted by the pheromones or the lost and loving looks of those he struck, but Willow had changed all of that. His mother was already furious with him for not making her fall in love with Kevin, one of Aphrodite's never-ending suitors, and for his complete withdrawal from the human realm. Kevin was dead now, which satisfied Eros to no end. His mother had done it, and he felt no guilt for her actions. A misplaced log and a swerve—and Aphrodite had her revenge. He was in no way sorry. Kevin had damaged and humiliated the woman Eros loved. He deserved far more than the instant death his mother had provided.

How could he continue to shoot his arrows when the only woman he desired was hurting and tormented? He withdrew to lick his own wounds and to deprive his mother of her powers. If it weren't for her insecurity, this never would have happened. *What a selfish, insecure woman she is!* Eros pounded his fist into the nearest tree, but there was no pain in her temple or gardens. Only the pain of the brokenhearted could be felt here. *Damn her—and damn her damn temple!*

His manipulative mother had a history of interference in love if she approved or not. She was vain and jealous, but Eros had no intention of letting her get her way again. He watched patiently as Flyn tried his best to break the bond that held Willow and Eros together, but Eros knew that no greater bond existed than what he had with Willow. He may have asked a few of his fairy or brownie friends to misplace things in Willow and Flyn's ramshackle home in hopes of causing problems. It seemed to work more often than not, and as they argued more and made up less, Eros felt his moment of victory coming soon. He would have the love he chose. Regardless of Aphrodite's opinion, he would have Willow—or no one would.

CHAPTER 12

After gassing my car up and studying the map in detail, I drove south at a reasonable speed. I had never left the state of New York and had no idea what the South would be like. I knew I had a good twenty-four-hours ahead of me, but I had no idea what I would be introduced to. I expected my sister to be living in a commune that was similar to ours, but I realized I only knew a few tidbits my parents had passed along. Most of the time, I was only pretending to listen.

As I drove away from the Eastern Seaboard, I was enamored by the size of the trees I began to pass. Huge pine forests lined each side of the hilly interstate highway. I saw cypress and oaks that were larger than any I had ever seen. I stopped briefly in West Virginia to refuel and resupply my small cache of food and water, get oil, and fix a flat since my old Toyota wasn't a top-notch car. It had almost two hundred thousand miles on it. It had never let me down before, but I didn't know what could happen in twenty-four hours of road time. It had rarely been driven outside of a hundred-mile radius of my parents' home.

At the travel station, I bought a bundle of CDs since I couldn't find a radio station that wasn't gospel or country music—neither of which would be my preference for a long trip. I'd had enough of talk radio and the news when I stopped, and I would have bought anything even remotely popular.

The service station attendant came out to pump my gas, and I was flabbergasted. I'd never experienced the full-service treatment and was astonished when he refused my tip. He said, "It's just paht of our sehvice here, ma'am."

I thanked him and found my tongue twisted around the extra syllables in his sentence as well as my own. I dragged out the words, making them match his syntax and worked on smiling with my full mouth. I waved toward pedestrians and drivers as I left. I liked the friendliness of the South and began to relax into a slow crawl toward Texas. It felt like an interminable crawl to a place of refuge from my past life and the curse it carried with it.

When I could drive no longer, I pulled over at a neglected viewing point on the side of the highway. I locked my doors and leaned my uncomfortable seat back to take a short break. I found myself in Eros's world as soon as my eyelids shut. It could have been any dream, but I was completely unaware that I had fallen asleep.

I saw him in a palatial setting. The primary color around him was white, but women of all ages, races, builds, and colorings waited on him hand and foot. As I watched through my dream mind, I saw him suggestively eye the women around him, but by and by, he turned each one down, even to the most beautiful brunette I had ever seen with almond-shaped eyes the color of the kudzu I'd seen on the road. I woke up confused and panting, not knowing where I was. As my breathing steadied, I rolled by shoulders and stretched in the confines of my Toyota. Yawning, I pointed my tires toward Texas in the hopes that my sister could answer some of my questions. We had never been close due to the age difference and her living outside the commune, but I prayed she could answer my questions better than Bren could.

I arrived in her neighborhood on one of the hottest afternoons in the history of Fort Worth. It was a ghastly hundred degrees, and a light rain made the air thick. I felt like I was breathing underwater. I stopped to refuel and ask for directions to the address from the birthday card, I found the air harder to breathe. I felt like I'd been submerged in the ocean.

Her address was incredibly easy to find. I followed the directions and printed instructions the gas attendant and an older gentleman customer had provided me. I was awestruck by the flatness of the place. Having spent so much time driving recklessly over valleys, mountain ranges, hills, and deep ravines, I felt trapped in a shallow bowl that extended as far as I could see.

I became utterly lost as I drove. Nothing looked different from anything else. As I scanned her neighborhood, I searched for anything that would give me an idea where the commune was located. I looked for a water tower, a windmill, or a garden, but nothing looked like where we had grown up.

Another roadside consultation of the map and directions revealed that I was very close. I was more comfortable finding my way on foot. I found an empty spot on a side street that assured me the parking was free. I grabbed my two small bags and my purse and headed in the direction of my sister's place.

Chapter 13

The flat sidewalk was devoid of any leaves or trash. I felt the hot, humid air closing in around me. Life there seemed to be mixed with vivid artificial greens and the gray and black of hot asphalt and concrete. Flowers bloomed, and houses were painted in different colors, but I only saw green, gray, and black. I only heard the slap of my shoes on the sidewalk. I couldn't understand my anxiety even though I was showing up on my sister's doorstep half a country away from where I lived. She was still my sister, and surely my parents had read my note.

I blamed my breathing difficulties on the claustrophobic feeling of so many similar houses on the street. I had visited neighborhoods like it before, but my eyes darted back and forth, waiting for someone or something to pop out from behind the immense oak and pear trees along the sidewalk. I tried to take deep breaths to calm my pounding heart, but the air was too thick. It was painful. I regretted not leaving the bags in my car, but it was too late to worry.

It was so quiet. I felt as though my footsteps would disturb the solitude my sister and her husband had chosen. No one heard my flapping feet entering the suburban bliss or the pounding of my heart as I struggled to breathe. The scent in the air would have been delightful if my trip hadn't been hasty. I had no idea what to expect when I showed up at Rose's doorstep.

I arrived after five minutes of dragging my feet and my bags. Perspiration covered my face and arms. My hands were slick on the handles of my bags. As I spied a mailbox with the numbers I was looking for, I glanced across the street. Modern, single-level brick homes and two-story homes lined the street. They all looked strangely similar. I had never seen a neighborhood so quiet and devoid of life. The mailboxes were lined up on one side of the street, and most of the houses did not have corresponding numbers on the faces of the houses or in the front yards. I had no idea where to begin to look since I had never seen a picture or heard any descriptions of my sister's home.

I was tempted to turn and flee to the safety of my car, but as I dropped my bags to wipe the sweat from my forehead with my sleeve, the front door of the house directly across from me opened. A snappy dog raced across the lawn, barking furiously at me. I was stunned when my sister stepped out and yelled, "Charlie! Charlie! Get your ass back here this minute or no treats for you!"

I stood there with my mouth was open, ready to call out.

"Charlie! Get back here this minute!"

As the words reverberated through my mind, the sharpness of them tugged at my heart.

When she yelled for the dog again, I remembered that her husband was also named Charlie.

I hid behind a low limb on a pear tree, and the dog darted across the street. It began scratching and whimpering at the edge of the tree-lined walkway. I knew the dog could smell me even if it was blind, but it never came closer than the curb.

My sister screamed, "Charlie! Get back here or you'll live to regret it!"

I glanced around the tree to look at the furry animal.

The dog's pleading eyes looked remarkably like her husband's eyes. It put me on edge, and I glued my body behind the tree until I could see nothing of her house.

The dog stood at attention, unable or unwilling to continue to the sidewalk where I was trying desperately to hide. I don't know why I chose to stay hidden, but I couldn't think of anything else at the moment.

"Charlie! Now! Or you will regret it!" Her words echoed through the neighborhood.

Charlie turned in a quick circle, looked over his hind end with a pleading look, tucked his tail, and began to stroll toward my sister's front door. He never looked back, and my sister gave him a sharp kick in the rear as he crossed her threshold.

I was dumbstruck by what I had heard and seen. I wondered who my sister was and why she was living so far away from anything that resembled our commune with a dog named after the man she had married. I crumpled to the ground with my back against the tree, facing away from the house. My bags were scattered around me. I'm not sure how long I sat there, but I couldn't manage to haul my bags back to the car. I hadn't brought that much with me, but my arms felt like they couldn't possibly aid me off the ground—much less pick up those bags. I took a deep breath, closed my eyes, and wrapped my weary arms around my knees. I had to think, I had to eat, and I had to get some sleep. I had no doubt about it. I shook my head to clear the cobwebs and tried to figure out the puzzle.

Nothing came to me. *Why would my sister lie to us all?* She had told us she was living happily in a commune with her slightly older but still handsome husband. They wanted to have children soon but had been unsuccessful in that endeavor. I couldn't wrap my mind around what was going on. I sat under the tree. The only signs of life were a few distant squirrels and some birds.

Why did she lie to us? Should I still pop in unexpected? I assumed my parents would have warned her of my arrival to assure themselves that I had arrived safely. After seeing my sister screaming at Charlie and chastising the dog for crossing the road, I knew she had no idea about my arrival. I took a deep breath and smelled ivy and honeysuckle. I knew it wasn't honeysuckle season, but didn't consider the alternatives. I needed to think. No other person crossed my path.

If my parents had any idea about where my sister was living, they never mentioned it in front of me.

Saddened and depressed, I pushed myself off the ground onto wobbly legs and took another breath. I grabbed the slick handles of my bags and trudged back to my car. Fatigue was my only partner at that point, and I just needed to sit down.

No answers to my problems could be found there from what I had seen and heard. I wasn't about to make my presence known after all I had experienced in that bizarre neighborhood. *Have I completely lost my mind? Has my sister? Have we all?*

I stored my bags in the car and put my hands together on the steering wheel. Eventually, my eyes began to water from exhaustion. I finally closed them and rested my forehead against my arms. I needed to rest for a moment—and then I could make peace with where I was and what I was doing there.

CHAPTER 14

"Mother, you have no idea what you're saying! This is all my fault. Willow had nothing to do with this accident, and Psyche certainly didn't! She has been gone forever!" Eros could tell by the look on his mother's face that she wasn't sold on any of it. "Please, Mother? I won't allow her to run around the world looking for answers that she will never find, especially from those horrid sisters of hers. You've known them forever. You must understand!"

Aphrodite stared at him with her beautiful gaze and instructed her nymphs to play louder and bring more food and wine. She reclined delicately in a chaise that a renowned European sculptor made for her. It formed to her body perfectly, as if she were suspended by loving hands.

Her eyes, as they turned toward him, were everything except loving. Her gaze was icy and he finally was forced to look away and down, avoiding the accusation in that look.

After a servant brought her wine, cheese, and fruit, she sighed loudly. "Oh, Ares, do you see what being a hopeless romantic has done to our fair son?" She reclined further, looking up. When no answer came, she sipped her wine and ate a small piece of fruit.

"Mother, just tell me what is wrong with this woman so I can understand what is going on with us all."

No answer.

Aphrodite nibbled away as if he had never spoken, and his frustration with her was reaching a boiling point. With his bow and quiver by his hip, he felt the fire from his arrows warm with each exasperating sentence. It was worse with the ones she didn't say. As he was becoming more annoyed by her lack of response, he had a wild desire to draw and nock one of his arrows and shoot her directly though whatever heart she had remaining in that shallow chest of hers. He loved his mother, but he had never met anyone who was as disillusioned as the goddess of love. His gut twisted when he compared his beautiful Willow to his evil, spiteful mother. He dared not look anywhere but directly at the space in front of him or between his whitened knuckles that he clasped together. He held them there to keep from throttling her in the temple.

Just as he was about to give up any hope of strategizing with her or strangling her, an odd whoosh sounded as if a window had blown open. As her handmaidens disappeared, his ears popped like a storm was blowing in. As soon as he realized nothing of the sort could be possible on Olympus, he looked up and saw the dashing, massive figure of his father.

"Cupid, uh, I mean Eros, uh … Ah, hell, who changes their name after thousands of years?" Clearing his throat, he began again.

Aphrodite sat up on the chaise and looked as seductive as possible.

"Son! What is with all this nonsense? I understand the desire to be with a human woman with all their breathlessness for life and their desire to please a god or even a demigod, but you and your mother need to agree on a safe and sound way to make her yours and allow her to forget! It's as easy as that!" Ares said as he lounged casually against a column.

"Father!" Eros shouted.

"I will never allow that to happen!" she screamed.

Eros turned on his heel to leave the vast space and heard a distinct chuckle. Angered beyond his imagination, Eros whirled around. He nocked and aimed an arrow before the turn was complete. "You

vile and hateful gods have no say in whom I love!"
Anger rippled through the space separating them.

Aphrodite looked mildly surprised, but Ares
showed no reaction. He was stunned by his
emotions, spun on his heel, and left them to fight it
out on their own.

CHAPTER 15

Eros knew quite well when I was sleeping since he visited me so often in my dreams. I had basically given up on seeing him in the physical realm, but I was elated to see him in my dreamscape.

He came to me a few minutes after I went to sleep. Holding me in his arms, he whispered, "Willow, I have no place that I would rather be than here with you!"

I knew there was a "but" in there somewhere, but I couldn't fathom what it meant. I relaxed into his arms as he held me against his chest.

Caressing my jaw, cheek, and neck, he kissed me with everything he had.

I kissed him back just as desperately. We held each other, and I felt a passion I had never known. My body felt as if it were on fire from my toes up, and my belly clenched as I kissed him.

I turned my sleeping eyes to look into his and was shocked at the passion that filled them. I was also truly shocked—as in electricity. A volt passed through my body that would have woken a zombie.

My eyes popped open, and I was alone in my car. The slight scent of ivy and flowers wafted through my open window. As I jolted awake, I saw the last of a jagged light in the sky, which was followed almost immediately by a loud boom. My ears popped painfully, and I gazed out my front window. I'd been awakened so suddenly that it took me a moment to realize where I was. As I moved my eyes sleepily around the ideal neighborhood, I felt the sheen of sweat on my face. I realized where I was.

Almost as soon as the recognition hit me, sirens came blaring around the corner. Apparently there was a fire! As my eyes focused on my surroundings, fire trucks, ambulances, and police cars screamed past me, lights and sirens blazing, in full rescue mode.

Like everyone else in the neighborhood, I ducked out of my seclusion to find out what the heck had happened. I turned the corner to find every blinking light nestled as closely as they could get to my sister's house. It looked like a war zone. Scraps of furniture and linens were scattered across her tree-lined boulevard. The house that had stood on a tiny section of similar homes had been leveled. I was in complete shock as neighbors and rescue workers rushed by me. No one noticed or questioned my presence, and everyone pressed forward to see the ruins.

My sister's house was a total loss. Not another single house on the block, or as far as I could see, had been touched. There was no rain falling and no storm brewing.

My mouth was wide open. I couldn't think. My mind had gone numb—and so had my body.

A warm hand gently rested on my shoulder, and I felt myself being pressed into a thick carpet of grass. I plopped down on the grassy lawn, and it jarred me into the moment.

When I looked up, a distinguished gentleman in his forties or fifties was staring down at me. "Have a seat, Willow … before you fall down."

I stared at my knees and clasped my hands tightly around them. I looked up momentarily, searching for the face that knew my name. The light blinded me for a second.

He moved to block out the rays from the lights sprinkling through the trees. "Head between your knees. Breathe deep and long. It will help." He spoke softly but with authority.

I did as he said, and as the firefly lights behind my eyes began to disappear, it dawned on me where I was. I remembered the circumstances that had brought me there.

I looked toward the spot my sister's lovely home had stood and was discouraged to see a firefight going on that no one could have survived. I was speechless as I turned to face my rescuer.

His golden eyes were kind. The crinkles at the edges made me feel like I knew him. He patted my back and whispered noises of comfort that needed no translation.

My sister and I had never been close, and after my experience earlier, I doubted we ever could be. Still, I was in shock.

What will I tell my parents? What will I tell anyone? What happened here and why? Who is this man? And where is Eros?

Chapter 16

Aphrodite paced around her large room and fumed from Eros's debacle in Texas. If anger and failure could catch fire, it would have shot from her nostrils. He was not supposed to visit that vile human girl in her dreams, but she knew he did almost every night. He was becoming quite the night stalker, and she was determined to do something about it. The nasty vixen couldn't be refined enough to sleep in a bed. How was she to know that her sister either turned her away or couldn't bear to be under the same roof?

Aphrodite understood siblings and the rivalry involved. *Look at her family—and tell me there aren't problems getting along. Sure, happily ever after exists just like fairies and five-leaf clovers. Both do, but they are rare and misunderstood.* When the goddess of love no longer believes, the mortal and magical worlds are in for some pain. Most of the time, she detested her brothers and sisters, but once in every great while, it came in handy to have a few gods and goddesses to call upon for favors or the collection of a favor owed.

She kept a tight, stingy eye on who owed whom and for what reason. The thought made her chuckle, but she was in no mood to be humored. Her other children were usually handy to manipulate—even Eros when he wasn't smitten. Phobos, Aphrodite's daughter, was especially useful as she could instill fear in even the most courageous.

She loved Phobos's idea of making Charlie appear as a dog. He was smelly and horrid and married to the awful Rose. A witch is all she was and not a very good one at that! Rose actually once thought that she could gain Ares's attention by giving him magical weapons that she and that sap husband, Charles, crafted.

Aphrodite made sure he'd never seen a single gift. The lame witch deserved to die—even if she had missed her preferred target! Dammit!

She thought the dog was a novel idea. That awful man deserved to be a dog after he married that equally horrible sister of the oh-so-beautiful Psyche.

"Willow. Her name is Willow! Damn her!" she said.

"Yes, mother." Eros jerked around to find him glaring at her just inches away with hate and fire in his eyes. He had snuck up on her in her temple. *Unthinkable!*

She couldn't help but notice how beautiful he was standing there. He looked so much like his father, Ares, especially after just thinking of him.

Eros gripped her arms, shook her violently, and whispered, "Willow. Her name is Willow—and don't ever forget it." He released her so suddenly that she fell to the marble floor.

She was unhurt but still ashamed and jealous. "Son!" she screamed. "If you leave now, don't ever come back!"

He met her spiteful glare and turned to face her.

She lifted her chin and straightened her spine on the white floor.

"Don't worry! I never want to see your putrid self again! It isn't all about being beautiful, Mother," Eros said. "Words are heavy, Goddess! Beware how you use them. They can cut, inflict fear, and cause laughter and tears. Heavy words and heavy love mean something. It requires you to be good and kind and loyal. Not that you'll ever know!" He walked out without even closing the door.

The noise and the open door invited her servants and muses to look in on her. They tried to assist her to her lounge, but she screamed at all of them as she rose to her feet. "Get out now!"

They picked up their dresses, heels clattering against the floor, and dashed out with her stomping behind them.

Aphrodite slammed the door as hard as she could manage, still feeling shaky from Eros's anger, and stalked to a wall of mirrors. Yanking her fingers through her hair and smoothing her dress, she looked at her reflection and tried desperately to soothe herself. What she saw astonished her to the core. She saw a woman with wrinkles? *What? How can that be?* Her mouth was set in a grim line and tiny lines the size of fairy bones creased her lips. She saw an unsightly line between her eyebrows, but her hair and body where still perfect. Turning her back on the image, she flung herself in the lounge and yelled, "Dionysus! Now!"

Crossing her arm over her eyes, she rested while she waited. *This could take a while.* She knew he would appear. She would bask in her misery while she waited. She stomped her foot and yelled for music and wine. Both appeared immediately.

CHAPTER 17

"Oh, Psyche, how I wish you were here. You were the strongest and most loyal of us all. My mother is as awful as always! She could never compete with your beauty or your perseverance and love. They call that bitch the goddess of love? That was you, my darling. Always you. I never thought I could love another after our life together. I had no idea, but I've been alone for so long. I'm lonely, and I miss you. I miss our life. I miss being loved and loving with my whole heart. I miss ... Willow? My body feels like a prison. I can't stay away. I don't know what to do."

Heart throbbing in his chest, Eros sighed, relieved at the honesty he had finally voiced—even if no one heard but a ghost and his own soul. He sprawled out further.

"You would like her. She has spunk and powers that she's unaware of that speak for her purity and her soul. She doesn't persuade or manipulate people even if it would mean a much easier life for her if she did. She has the power to manipulate anyone if she chooses, but she loves so much, like you did … before. Dear gods, I can't keep this up. Please, darling? Please understand. Psyche, my love, you need to let me know you understand. I'm broken."

Eros lay on his back in a field of poppies. His mind swirled with love, hatred, and the deep scent of the fields. It was hard to decipher memories from dreams and hope for a future. Willow had never reminded him of Psyche. That was one of the things he had loved about her from the beginning. Psyche was as dark as Willow was light. Psyche had been innocent and naive in the beginning just like Willow, but Psyche had to experience trials that no woman deserved simply to prove her love. It matured her. She grew wise from the experiences but also harder. As the strongest-willed and most loving person on earth, she had earned her way into his life. He didn't regret it. It required his mother to concede a victory to her mortal daughter-in-law. He had loved her strength and only rarely missed the innocence of youth. When it dawned on his foggy mind that Aphrodite was at it again, he said, "Damn that blasted woman!"

He knew in his heart that words had weight. They were heavy, and they meant different things to different people at various times. In a life of words, they can cut and harm or love and charm. *They're lies and truth.* He couldn't comprehend why she would care. He recalled the River Styx and the reformation of life. He knew the tests and trials of the underworld, but it had been a long time since he had rested. *Could it be? Does my mother know? Is she keeping it from me?* His eyes melted with a forlorn thought that he had been used again and left wanting by his own mother.

He slept. And as gods often do, he traveled in his sleep.

CHAPTER 18

Willow drove hard toward Oklahoma. She didn't see or hear anything for several hours. She headed north toward her last and only hope for help. The landscape changed, and pine forests gave way to flat fields of scrub grass and twisted, wind-blown oaks.

Lily is far and above my parents' favorite. We all know it, so it really isn't a big deal. My parents love us all, and that's what matters. Lily married an oilman in Oklahoma when I was too young to remember, but my sweet, humble mother can't stop talking about their success. Bren is always reading her letters and e-mails to us. *Lily and Pete did this and went here and bought whatever.*

It was hard to imagine my mother being impressed until my mind flashed back to our shopping trip in the city. I realized that my mother did miss certain aspects of life outside of the commune, which was why she went on and on about Lily. I barely know her, but Bren acts like she hung the moon. She hadn't been to visit in years, but my parents spent a long camping trip with Pete and

Lily when I was eleven or twelve. I stayed behind, but my father was upset when Pete lost his wallet in the lake. It had all of their money in it. Bren never let my father finish his grumbles regarding the trip, but I'm not aware of the outcome. It was the last trip they ever took together. Lily only called on special days, and Pete never called or e-mailed. I could barely form a picture in my mind of them, and when I caught a flash of memory, I knew it was outdated.

I didn't have a recent card from Lily to guide my way to her home, but I knew she lived in Pittsburg County, Oklahoma, just south of Tulsa. It was a pretty straight drive north, and I could have seen for miles if I had been looking. I just planned on getting as close as possible and asking around for my rich brother-in-law or using a phone book somewhere. How hard could it be to find a redecorated, white Victorian in this flat space under the name of Peter Lumpy?

I was utterly spent and exhausted, but I didn't dare stop to rest. A simple long blink could become a never-ending night filled with dreams of Eros and waking nightmares that rocked me into the next day. I didn't dare risk even a short nap.

As I drove through the vast flatlands of Oklahoma with hills and outcrops on either side, I tried to figure out what had happened in Fort Worth. My sister and the life she had built were completely swept off the face of the earth. If I thought about it, I would lie down right here and never get up. All I could do was press ahead and hope to find some kind of solace—away from Eros and this stupid curse.

I needed answers, and I needed them soon.

CHAPTER 19

I pulled into Pittsburg County, Oklahoma, just before noon, and it was blazing with heat. Everywhere I looked, there were shimmers off the asphalt. I couldn't explain the fog over the town. It was as if everyone in the county had been burning their fields, homes, and trash all at one time. The smell was putrid and burned my eyes.

My complete exhaustion and refusal to sleep didn't help the matter, but I was on a mission. No matter the situation, I had to tell Lily what was going on. I knew in my heart that Rose's death was on my shoulders, and I needed to be the one to tell Lily since they had always been closer in age and temperament.

The county seat was small and desolate, but I felt that I was in the right place.

As parched as I was, I zeroed in on the nearest soda sign I saw, hoping for a drink and directions.

The place was gray wash blue and was covered in neon signs in English and Spanish. It wasn't much to look at for sure, but the fans turning at full blast inside and the promise of a wet mouth and an empty bladder forced me to drag my weary legs in that direction. My eyes were so heavy that the dry, hot wind didn't affect my focus on the store and some answers.

Even if I had terrible news to share, my desire to find answers drove my aching body forward.

I slowly crossed the gravel parking lot and was embraced by a rush of cool air as the most massive man I had ever seen held the door open for me. After so many hours of heat and weariness, the open door felt as if I were approaching the gate of heaven. I glanced at the man holding the door, and my mind focused on cooling off and taking a nice, long pee. He winked at me in passing, but the next moment, I was engulfed in the modern world of air-conditioning. The past seventy-two hours of my life disappeared into a commercial-sized air filter.

I could only stand, breathe, and mop my face with a shredded piece of old napkin.

I looked around and saw grunge upon grunge. Dirty men in a dirty place looked at me like they would an alien that was on fire. As long as I could breathe again, everything was fine.

Once I gained my senses from the Freon breeze blowing in my face, I pivoted toward the ladies' room with a mission. I spent fifteen minutes in chicken-fried-smelling heaven as I used the facilities to wash my hands and my face. I ran my wet hands through my greasy hair and pushed it back into its original ponytail.

When I returned to the store, I was refreshed. I felt like I had a new lease on life. Even with the exhaustion of the drive, I felt ready to get to my sister. I hoped we could come to some kind of relationship and prepare to tell our parents about Rose and Charlie—if they didn't know already.

I walked toward the cashier with a weak smile and filthy clothes. I could feel the leering eyes of three dirt-crusted men as I made my way past the candy and chips. Out of nervousness, I grabbed a bag of Funyuns and headed to check out and get some directions.

"Howdy? Is the all for you today, ma'am?" The clerk had a strange, lilting uplift to each question he asked.

"That's all? And maybe some directions if you don't mind me asking." *Why am I doing this? I'm going crazy!*

"Sure, ma'am. What can I help you find?"

I explained that I was looking for my sister and her husband to pass on some terrible news.

The young man looked more puzzled than I thought possible and then let out a huge back-bending belly laugh. "You think any big oilmen live in this backwoods town? Dang, girl? Where the heck are you from? Ain't nobody here but miners, old miners, those too messed up to mine, and yours truly who runs the service station. There is my daddy, the sheriff, and a judge that's 'bout dead. Most women ran off at one time or another—but no rich oilmen!" He guffawed and punched another dirty man on the shoulder.

"Oilmen?" He snorted and slapped his buddy. He laughed hard and chucked his knee. "Rich oilmen? I'll be damned. Been asked for a lot of things, but that ain't one of them. Are you in the family way, honey, and looking for your old man?"

"Uh … no … I mean … no! It's not like that. I'm looking for my sister. She's married to an oilman in this county, and I have some dreadful news to give her. I mean if she's here. This was her last known address, and I came here to find her. Ugh. Maybe I'm in the wrong Pittsburg County. I've been driving a long time. Maybe I got lost?"

Stunned silence greeted my goofy grimace, and all I could do was glance at the eyes plastered to my stupid big mouth.

"There ain't no big oilmen round here, but if you tell me who you're looking for—how he looks maybe, what he drives—I'll be the man to show you. No man should leave a fine-looking lady like you in the family way without offering help. Even if he's in the prison down south of here. No, siree. My mama would skin me alive if she thought I didn't help ya out!"

"What? Wait? No. I'm not. It's not like that! I'm just looking for my sister and her husband. It's family—but not 'family way' like you are talking about. Just tell me if you know anyone named Pete and Lily Smith? I just need to find them … um … to give them news. That's my sister and her husband." I stumbled and fumbled and stood there, unable to look any of the men in the eye.

He scratched his whiskers and looked down at the dirty gray counter.

"Well, let's see here. Most the folks round here are either Smith or Jones on account of a felony here or a probation issue there. Let's see. Could you tell me what they look like?"

I blew her hair out of my eyes and glared at the idiot in front of me. "Look! You don't understand. My sister lives here with her husband in a beautiful restored Victorian house. It was on the Christmas house tour last year and took third place. I saw the photos. Surely you know where I'm talking about. You can call them and ask if they know me. Please. I've been on the road a really long time." I looked toward him with my biggest sad face, and he connected with my eyes.

I thought he would break down and tell me he was pulling my leg or something, but he slapped his knee again and went straight to the ground in the loudest belly laugh I'd ever heard come from anyone over the age of three.

My mouth fell open, and the tears I had been holding for so long streamed down my face, wetting the neck of my sweat-soaked shirt.

The next thing I knew, I was on a moldy mattress on the floor with a rag pressed to my forehead. I didn't know if I was dead and in hell or still alive in the boonies of Oklahoma. My eyes wouldn't open, and my mouth was drier than it had ever been. *Oh, hell. I'm still stuck in this crazy backwoods county with not one friend, no sister, no Eros, and no hope.*

As I drifted into my fitful semiconscious state, I felt lips press against my temple and linger there for a moment. My mind eased, and I finally slept. Without dreams or nightmares, I drifted off with a kiss in my head and grime in every part of my body. I was in heaven.

CHAPTER 20

I woke up an unknown amount of hours later to a gray ceiling, gray walls, and the smell of coal dust on every layer of my skin and clothes. The sun was weakly shining through the blinds on a gray, cloudy day. Whatever time it was, the day gave no hint except the incredible heat. I was grateful to still have my clothes when I remembered the leering gazes of the men at the store and what had transpired. *Where am I? How did I get here?* I pried my eyes open to the feeling of sand under my eyelids and didn't recognize a single thing.

"Oh, there you are my dehya," a voice said from a doorway that suddenly swung open. A small, portly, teapot of a woman came in with a tray of liquids and placed it heavily on the cabinet. She began tidying my bedding and checking my head for fever. Horns? I'm not too sure, but she was thorough. I had never seen this woman before, and without the moisture to form a single word, I was in no place to ask her where I was or who she was. She fussed around me a moment and then hustled back to the tray. She returned with a tall glass of golden liquid. She tilted it up, looked at it, and turned to me. "Just wat the daacter awed red. Sweht tee is tha necta' of the gawds, ya know? Heya now, bah-by, drank up!"

Huh? With no other choice but to die of thirst, I drank. Oh what sweet heaven that first sip was. I could barely swallow it at first, but as the sweet honey and the bitter tealeaves met my lips and tongue and wet my mouth, I agreed with this woman. I was drinking the nectar of the gods.

"Nah slow dawn there, hawny. You ain't wanting go get no stitch naw, are ya?" She moved the "mother's milk" out of my reach.

With a groan and a frown, I struggled my way up onto the moldy pillows.

"Thay're ya go, Willow, bahby. It's all gonna be fine. You gotcha sista Lils here ta take sohm goot care-a you."

I lost consciousness for the second time that day.

CHAPTER 21

I was dead asleep in a lumpy bed that smelled of mildew, hay, and some sort of campfire. I couldn't see the building around me with my eyes closed, but I felt a warm body next to me, breath on my neck, and an arm over my waist. I wasn't panicked or afraid. I snuggled in closer and felt a tiny pinprick on my hip. Rubbing it unconsciously, I hugged him closer, smelling his scent of ivy, honeysuckle, and the simple freshness like the outdoors on a spring day. It was amazing how well I knew him in my dreams, but I doubt I could have picked him out of a crowd of supermodels, gods, and demigods.

He was beautiful, but something more drew me to him. I felt my clothes sticking to my body, and my hair melted to my scalp. I sensed the breeze of spring moving across my skin. Tiny ripples of the softest kisses caused the hairs on my arms and neck to stand on end. I didn't speak a word—and neither did he—but I knew who he was. I basked in his comfort. "Eros?" my mind called. My lips said nothing because I was paralyzed from exhaustion.

Ocean waves filled my mind and whispered, "Shhh, darling. Sleep." He kissed my eyelids. "Rest. You need this. I'll be here when you wake up." I heard this repeatedly throughout the night. And I slept and slept.

When I awoke, it was to another gray day in the same gray room. He wasn't there, but I never really expected him to be. I didn't know if he had been there at all. Maybe I was having some amazing dreams, and I hadn't seen him at all. My mind was mush, and I had no idea if anything was real anymore.

The time had changed, but I had no idea how many hours I had been in bed or in the house. I had a vague recollection of a full moon behind my eyelids and the sunrise across my legs. I could barely remember where I was, and the idea that that woman was my sister was beyond any comprehension. An urgent need to go to the bathroom had me pushing against the pillows and pulling against the blankets to get myself into a seated position. My head swam, and my stomach flipped and tumbled. I weakly pulled myself up as far as I could and fell back with a whoosh against the sooty wall. I wedged my eyes open further with a finger and thumb on each hand and took in my surroundings. Unable to move an inch, I did the only thing I could think of and began rapping on the wall above my head. I tried to draw attention to my full bladder and weakened state.

The door burst open with a flurry of large floral prints on a short, wide body. "Ah mya Lort? What've ah done to ya self, Willa? Ya needing somethin'?Well, let's jus have a look-see."

This large, small bundle of energy with a mane of massive blonde waves of hair to her waist and flowers covering every inch of exposed skin began fussing around my bed like a bumblebee.

"Pee," I said.

"Why, babay, that's all ya had to say. Let's get ya up now, bear wit me. Okay? You sure is lots bigger than the lasts time I done this fer ya. Das fer dam sure."

I would have liked to spend time studying this strange specimen of a woman pulling me out of bed, but nature called. She huffed and heaved me up to the edge of the bed. Once there, we both rested, breathing heavily and covered in soot and grime.

"Com'on, babay. I'll get ya to that potty and see ya cleaned up a little. Then I'll warsh them bedstuffs so I can get to cookin' dinnah fer the boys and Petie. Sure hope they dint keep ya from restin'!"

Dang, does this woman ever stop talking? If my teeth hadn't been floating, I would have had time to ask questions, but she carried me to a small hall closet that had been converted into an old-fashioned outhouse with an optional shower spray above the toilet and a huge drain and hose in the floor.

Stripping me down naked with two swipes of her hands in a crisscross action that had to have been practiced, she set me down on the toilet. Turning her back to gather up some things and leave me to my privacy—or so I thought—the one-sided conversation began again.

I let go of thirty-six hours of force-fed Popsicles.

"Ah, dahlin', Willa. Ya just can't be surprised enough to be me when you showed up here all passed out drunk in da broad daylight. No, no, we see plenny of that round here with the miners and all dem, but, Lort, whatcha thanking, girl? I got a reputation to uphold wit Petie being night foreman and all at da mines? He just barely got this raise cause the last boy dun blew off his thumb on a stick o' that new stuff. I can't have you caterwaulin' round here like some common trash now. Whatever was Mama thanking when she sent you here? Huh?"

Before I could answer, my bladder empty and my mind spinning and dizzy, she turned on me like an Olympic ice skater. She threw a sliver of soap at me and turned on the portable shower spray.

I sputtered with surprise, but the water was not very warm and smelled metallic. Once I caught the squeal in my throat, the feeling of the soot and the days in bed washing away was well worth any shock. Even my thoughts and memories of Eros seemed to swirl down the drain for a few silent seconds.

"Now, Wiila, ya gotta use that there soap for suds and that other there to wash off the suds cause this is damn hart water here. There's a clean towel here, but just the one and call me to crank the wrench real tight so it don't leak all night and make Little Pete Junior get up all night ta tinkle. Kay? Okay. Dang. I gotta cook some supper before those boys get here. Holler for me, and I'll find ya a nice dress to wear. Kay? Kay!"

And she was gone, leaving me in a closet with a toilet, a shower sprayer, and two kinds of soap. I had lived rough over the years, visiting friends and other communes, but this was a shock. I didn't know this woman, and I had no idea what my mother had been talking about for all those years.

Numbly, I soaped my skin until the water ran clear, and then I soaped it again. The mud forming in the drain almost had me losing the nothing in my stomach, but I forced myself to swallow. I ran an entire gallon of water straight from the spigot to my stomach. Once I had quenched my thirst, I rinsed by mouth, scrubbed my hands hard over my face to rid myself of any lingering grime, and turned off the water.

A drop from the leaking shower hit the muddy floor. I reached for the towel, but my arm was too weak. Wielding a wrench was unthinkable. Drying off as best I could from a seated position in this tiny room, I closed my eyes and felt the warmth of being clean and rested. I wondered again if my dream had been true.

Shaking my head, I stood and opened the closet door to the screaming and fighting of several male voices below. *What have I gotten myself into now?*

CHAPTER 22

I struggled back to the bedroom and found a set of clothes on the freshly made bed. The clean sheets still had a gray hue, and the clothes looked like they had arrived by a time machine. The smallest pair of granny panties I had ever seen and an eighteen-hour bra in a 32B were on top of a floral housedress and skid-proof socks.

Beggars can't be choosers. I dressed quickly and was glad to be clean and clothed. I brushed my teeth with a new toothbrush, drank another gallon of water that had been left out, and hurried down the stairs toward the sound of chaos and the smell of food. The kitchen had a massive table shoved up against the wall, a cook stove in the corner, and a solid chopping block in the center. There was bedding pushed up under a window, and I knew the room served more than one purpose.

Lily was flush up against the cook stove, stirring crazily, and boys were wreaking havoc everywhere I looked. They seemed to be the ages of twelve to one, but it was hard to tell because they never stopped moving. A man was working on a small laptop at the table.

"Well, look what the cat drug in!" Lily said.

The chaos and noise stopped, and every male face in the room turned to look at me. When the stillness came over them, I was surprised to see only five male faces and my sister staring at me. The boys looked like mini versions of their mother: blond hair, blue eyes, full faces, and round bodies.

As we took each other in, I realized they were very close in age and size. No wonder it was hard to tell them apart.

Lily shook the wooden spoon and said, "Pete and Juniors, this is my sister, Willow. Willow, meet Pete and the Juniors."

Pointing at each boy, she said, "Meet Junior One, eight years old. Junior Two is six. Junior Three is four. Ha ha. I love saying that. And Junior Four is almost three, but ain't he great? Four boys in five years? Who'd a thought it?"

I was stunned and tongue-tied, but I said, "What? Why didn't Mom and Dad ever say anything? What's going on?" I couldn't believe my eyes.

"Oh, I never told Bren about the boys. Why should I? She's only interested if I have girls to put up for the gods, right?" She chuckled.

I felt sick to my stomach and dizzy.

Pete Senior saw my color fade, reached out, and grabbed my arm. As my legs failed me, he plopped a chair under me. I let my head hang between my knees and took deep breaths.

Four pairs of young male eyes bore into my skull. Pete Senior went back to work as if nothing had happened, and my sister stirred away at dinner like a madwoman.

CHAPTER 23

The next morning arrived early and bright. Heavy boots pounded the stairs, and my sister's shrill morning voice shouted at the boys to slow down.

I realized I hadn't dreamed for the first time in months. What did that mean? Had he given up? Was I finally away from his awful spell? Had I driven myself into an alternate universe? (That seemed as likely as any, especially with the noise and screaming going on below). I was better rested than I had been in months and had energy to burn. When I walked downstairs, my lungs filled with soot. I began to cough.

"Ah, we won't be having any of that there lungey cough going on 'round here now Willa! We ain't no wimps here in this minin' house, no siree!"

Mining? "You're miners? What do you mine? I've never heard a word about it." I stumbled out into the kitchen/bedroom, and four pairs of big blue eyes rested on me.

"Why we're the world's oldest coal miners ... in Oklahoma anyway! And damn proud of it!" She guffawed. "Now, boys, get your lights and helmets and come on."

The boys moved as she suggested.

"Willa, you want to go with us—or you won't to stay home today? You can't stay home many days as we'll be needin' the money to support ya, but I suppose—"

"I want to go!" I said. I don't know why I spoke up or why I said I wanted to go to the coalmine, but I did.

The boys became a flurry of activity as their mother directed them in outfitting me for the day's work. I was insulated in coveralls, wool socks, boots that almost fit, goggles, and a scarf in no time at all. The activity around me left me dizzy and hungry. A biscuit with sausage was shoved into my hand, and a warm coffee mug was pushed into the other as I was guided out into the very early morning sunshine. It was the best thing I had ever tasted. I felt alive and somehow in control for the first time in months. Finally, I had a day's work ahead of me and a full belly. Then, I remembered that I had yet to tell Lily about Rose and Charlie's house blowing them to smithereens. *Damn, life sucks.*

We got to the coalmine, and it was a bustling. I couldn't believe my eyes. The youngest and smallest boys were outfitted in scaling harnesses and lighted helmets. Before I could register what was happening, the boys jumped down a cable into a hole in the mountain. I caught a glimpse of my sister. She was smiling with pride and pumping her fist in the air. I shook my head to clear my vision and realized it didn't help at all.

After the children descended into the mountain cavern, the adults lined up to plunge to the middle of what seemed like hell. They were boisterous and excited as they scaled down into the earth. My sister was third to last in line, and I walked up to her.

She said, "You're staying topside today, Willa. No use you gettin' hurt so soon. You just rest easy and lay low. We'll be back soon."

"I have something to tell you about Rose, Lily. She had her house blown up—and I think it was my fault!"

"Ah, Willa, don't worry about a thing. We'll have time to talk once I'm topside again. Don't you worry about Rose and Charlie. They'll be just fine as long as they don't have no daughters!"

Before I could question her further, she grabbed the rope, clasped her harness, and jumped into the hole in the mountain. I was left above as the whole family went below.

Chapter 24

I stood at the mouth of the cavern and watched the pulleys carry my family into the abyss below. I had visions of the darkness of the mine, and I was terrified for a moment. I realized that was what they did. Every day, they did it, and everything seemed to be running well.

I was shuffled aside by other workers and went to lean against a lone tree that was stripped of leaves. It was so dry and desolate that I quickly realized the importance of my scarf. I wiped my eyes and nose, and it came away covered in grime. I could feel the heat coming off the mine, and the air was heavy with grit. I thought I felt the tree shift slightly behind me, but I put it off to my dizziness and the lack of oxygen up here.

"I'd hoped I would find you here," a deep male voice said from behind me. I should have been startled, but I knew that voice—and it felt like home.

I blew my nose, wiped my eyes, and turned to face Flyn. He looked absolutely heavenly! I rushed to him and threw my arms and legs around him.

He laughed deeply and held me close. His laugh was welcoming and the best medicine I had in forever. It was the happiest I had been in a very long time. I nearly laughed to death.

"Hey there, baby. You need to calm down before we both fall off this damn hillside. It's good to see you." He kissed me again—deeper and with more tongue. "Mmm," he said in a singsong voice that I knew so well. I held onto him with everything I had, and he groped my ass as he lowered me to the earth.

"What in the world are you doing here?" I practically yelled with a grin the size of the Grand Canyon. I was bouncing on my toes and could barely keep my hands off of him. I hadn't had time to realize how much I had missed him. I had so much to tell him.

He grabbed my hands and bent down to take in my eyes. He always made great eye contact, and his eyes looked like melted chocolate. I groaned out loud.

Flyn smiled and then grew serious. "Willow, sweetie, you need to listen to me and hear what I have to say."

I looked up into his gorgeous eyes and nodded like a complete idiot.

"There's been a terrible accident, and Rose and Charles have been killed. Your mother is very ill, and your father is up to his eyeballs in caring for her. He isn't doing well without her. You need to come home and bring Lily with you to help him out. I'm so sorry to be bringing such painful news." He hugged me hard, and his scent was perfectly Flyn and perfectly … not what I wanted. How could this wonderful, warm human man compete with a god that I had never seen in real life? It should be so easy to be with Flyn. I wanted it so much.

Why was I living in a dream world where I wasn't welcome or wanted instead of falling to my knees to worship this perfect male specimen in front of me? My stomach rolled, and my heart lurched. Apparently it showed on my face.

Flyn reached out and grabbed my elbows. In that very moment, the whole earth rocked and swayed beneath us. We both fell to our knees, and Flyn grabbed me. He held me close, covering me with his body. The explosion and dust ate up the remainder of the oxygen in the atmosphere, and I felt myself drift off again.

I woke up in a cubicle with dozens of nurses and aides rushing here and there. The place was a madhouse and seemed to be at full capacity.

Periodically, a doctor would saunter in and pick up a chart. Until he headed out, the nurses and candy stripers would get out of his way and look away deferentially. Whatever was going on was a big deal—and I seemed to be part of it.

Nurses came in and took my vitals, but if they asked me questions, I couldn't hear them over the intense ringing in my ears. My eyes were washed out, and various scrapes were dressed with gauze. My injuries were minor except for my hearing loss. I couldn't get my questions across about my sister, her family, or Flyn. No matter what I said, my hand was patted. I was tucked in and medicated. I heard nothing but the persistent whistle in my ears.

It took forever for the doctor to appear with an ear speculum and a large needle. He punctured my eardrum and drained the fluid. The pain was incredible, but the relief was worth it. I could finally hear again.

I asked the questions I had been holding onto, but I already knew most of the answers. My sister and her entire family were unaccounted for, and Flyn was on a critical care unit a floor above me.

I breathed a sigh of relief that he had survived and sobbed into my pillow for the loss of the family I had just recently found. I must have cried myself to sleep because I woke up to a horrible hangover of bruises and heartache only to be injected again to melt into silent oblivion.

Eros appeared in my opiate-induced dream state. He seemed to love being there and altering my train of thought. It was not very hard since I was pretty much out of it. He kissed me, held me, and apologized at least a thousand times. My heart melted, and he let me cry. My big tears wet his shirt and mine until I finally cried myself out.

I awoke the next morning, hurt and alone. I cried again.

CHAPTER 25

Aphrodite came unglued again. She railed and screamed and broke things in her temple. She ridiculed everyone around her and cursed her son to anyone who would listen.

"How could he do this to me again? The ungrateful son of Ares! I should have known that he would end up humiliating me again with his stupid crushes on mortal women!"

She smashed glassware and windows, threw sculptures into her furniture, and screamed, at the top of her lungs. Finally, exhausted, she threw herself on the floor and begged for help.

Help soon arrived, and it was just what she would have hoped for. Her family finally appeared to offer up redemption for all the favors she had granted them. She had friends on her side once again, and she meant to utilize whatever aid she had. Regardless of the cost, she would put an end to this obsession that Eros had and be done with this mortal bitch.

Eros wept in his room. He cried for his lost Psyche and for what Willow was going through. He understood the trials of loving a god—even a minor one—and felt the loss of her sisters. He felt her loneliness in the silence that followed the explosion. He felt her confusion about what had happened. It wrecked his thoughts and broke him to the bone. He inhaled the smell of poppies from his pillowcase and drifted off. When he felt a hand on his cheek, he impulsively moved toward it. He knew that smell and touch. He had known it for a millennium and would never forget it. He didn't think twice about his next move. He rolled over and reached for his beloved's face.

"No," she whispered.

Try as he might, his eyes wouldn't open. "Listen to me and hear my words, darling. Shhh. I'm here to tell you what you can do—but not what you have to do."

Eros tried to speak, but he was hushed again.

"Darling, I don't have much time, but I must tell you that you have to follow this through. You must go to Willow and convince her to choose you—or we will never be together again. Without this curse being fulfilled, I will never see you in the hereafter, and I need you here. I love you, and I miss you. Please do as you did with me—and damn your mother."

Eros woke up startled and groggy but with a mission in mind. He would stop at nothing until Willow was his—just as Psyche had been his.

CHAPTER 26

I was released from the hospital, but Flyn was still in ICU. He had a massive concussion but no lingering effects on his mind or memory. He greeted me with a smile and reached for me.

I took it and thumbed his knuckles as he looked into my eyes. Thank God my hearing had returned.

"I'm so glad you're okay," he said with a twinkle in his eye.

"You saved me!" My eyes filled with tears, and I rested my forehead on his hand.

"Oh, baby, you could have saved yourself. I was just your barricade. I'll always be your barricade when you need one."

I cried harder. This man I loved had risked his life for me. I cried for another lost sister and her boys—the ones she thought didn't require an introduction to our family. I cried for Eros and his dream visits. I missed him so much. I thought I would die! I was holding onto a living, breathing, beautiful man who loved me. *What the hell am I thinking?*

Flyn became stronger as the hours passed. Forty-eight hours after I was released, Flyn was ready to go home. I needed to get to my mother and help my father.

Flyn tried to make me leave earlier, but after he saved me, I felt that I owed him. He had given so much to me.

The day he was released from the hospital, we drove steadily down the interstate. I slept deeply and dreamed. I tried to make Flyn let me drive, but he recognized the bags under my red eyes and knew how long I had sat by his hospital bed.

I dreamed of Eros. We came together and made mad, passionate love over and over throughout the night as Flyn drove north toward what was left of my family. I don't know if I moaned in my sleep. Thank the gods that Flyn didn't mention it to me. I woke up sore, bruised, and more confused than ever. I was guilty of a crime I hadn't committed with my body as much as with my mind. I was red with embarrassment, but sweet Flyn just patted my hand and pulled over for gas and a break so we could change drivers.

After the third night of travel, I'd had enough. I crushed Flyn's pain pills in a glass of water. We stopped at a roadside hotel chain that was cheap and not very clean. Eros often drank from it during our nightly dream visits even though it was always full when I awoke. I had a perfectly clear vision in my mind of him drinking from my glass after an unusually intense lovemaking session. I had to hope and pray it would work. He had to take the bait because I just couldn't go on like that.

Chapter 27

Aphrodite hummed a sweet tune along with her musicians, sipped her red wine, and thought about Dionysus. Her temple had been set to right, and a plan had formed in her pretty little head. She would call in every favor ever owed her if it was the last thing she had to do.

Dionysus would come, most likely drunk and with woodland nymphs hanging all over him, but he would come. They had once been lovers—as had most gods and goddesses as far as Dionysus was concerned. He wasn't a picky god at all with all the wine at his fingertips. After all of his dalliances with mortal women, he owed her large!

She beckoned Persephone from the underworld. She would have to speak through Iris, which was always difficult in the underworld. Persephone owed Aphrodite for her son Adonis, and they both adored him. Persephone would make a deal as well.

Amazingly enough, Dionysus was the first to arrive. A nubile amazon woman clung to his arm. Twice his height and width, she was beautiful. He held a basket of what smelled like vomit under his arm. "What is it, Aphrodite? I was busy making chum beer. Why do you demand my presence here?" He slurred and stumbled through the simple sentence.

"I'm calling in my debt," she said sternly. "Now! This very moment! Get this whore out of my temple. I'll explain what you have to do!"

The massive woman disappeared in the blink of an eye. Dionysus, grinning slyly, struck a pose that would make any human male model want to slit his wrists.

"Not that kind of favor, Dio. Get over yourself. Get to earth now! Get my son drunk enough to make a fool out of himself, preferably in front of this pimple on his life, Willow. Make it quick and make it strong and maybe, just maybe, you'll have a favor coming from me!" She smiled seductively, allowing a glimpse of her long, shapely legs.

Dionysus, gulping loudly, turned and disappeared with a massive tent in the front of his pants.

Aphrodite giggled and fell back in her chaise, sipping wine and humming to the music. "The life of a goddess can be good." She drifted off to sleep.

As she slept, Persephone came to her dreams. *Ah, so much easier than iris messaging with the light and rainbows and all.*

Aphrodite loved Persephone much than any woman.

Persephone said, "I know what you want. And as much as I owe you, you know as well as I do that true love will always win."

"No!" screamed Aphrodite in her mind. "I will not let this leach have my son!"

"Oh, sweet friend, you asked for this when you made a mortal woman your enemy. She would have aged and died a gray, wrinkled thing, but you couldn't help sending Eros down there to ruin her life."

"No! Please help me. Help him."

Persephone sighed deeply. "Sister, I wish you luck, but I will never ply my trades as you. No matter what I owe you."

When Persephone was gone, Aphrodite bolted awake and wept for a long time.

CHAPTER 28

Willow made sure she had a couple of glasses of wine to make her sleepy. She finally resorted to taking an allergy tablet that she carried with her to make sure she was good and asleep, ready to dream away. She put the glass of water and narcotics on her bedside table and another on the floor on the other side of the bed. She certainly didn't want to be the one drugged, and Eros did make her awfully thirsty at night.

She brushed her hair and teeth and rubbed her favorite orange-scented lotion on her skin. She dressed in a way that she never did for bed. She wore a tight lace camisole and panties that left nothing to the imagination. Her normal T-shirt and sweats were discarded in the corner.

Flyn was sleeping in the room next door. He was still recuperating from his injuries. He had taken his medication and was down for the night.

While she washed her face, her eyes began to grow heavy. She knew the time was near. As she crawled into bed, she said a quick prayer that Eros would come and she would finally be able to trap him with the drugs and keep him near until she could figure out what the heck was going on with him. *Why does he only appear at night or in my dreams?* It was time for this to be resolved one way or another so she could finally get on with her life with Flyn or someone else who was actually there for her.

She still hurt from the loss of her sisters and worried desperately about her mother and father. She had to get to her mother and father. She could no longer play this nighttime game and maintain her sanity. It was time to stop it.

***

As Eros was leaving his mother's temple by the back door to avoid detection, he was shocked to find Uncle Dio beside a marble statue of himself. He was holding a large bladder of wine and two glasses. Dio always had wine aplenty, but Eros hadn't seen or sensed Dionysus in his mother's temple or grounds in a very long time. Dio and the goddess had a longstanding feud over the treatment of my brother. He had been poorly treated, and they had never gotten along after their brief affair. Dio never showed his face if he hadn't been beckoned, which should have been a clue. Eros could feel

Willow on the verge of sleep and needed to get to her as soon as possible.

"Are you sneaking out, child?" Dio said with the loud laugh of a drunkard. "Off to see a fair maiden or to wreak havoc on the poor mortals tonight perhaps?" He laughed even louder.

Uncle Dio could be a massive pain. He was propped up gallantly, looking fairly loaded with messy hair and red eyes.

"I'm just going out, Dio. Why in Hades has she called you here now? What have you done to anger the mighty Aphrodite this time?"

We never spoke against the goddess, especially on her own grounds because spies lurked behind every pillar and plant.

"Psh, I came to see you, son, not your mother. You know she's worried about you, and I can't say I blame her. I've loved many mortal women in my time, and it never turns out well. Always heartbreak, tears, and death. Here, join me in a toast."

No one can possibly say no to a toast from the god of wine. His wine was the sweetest nectar of the gods, and he was always talking about his relationships with mortal women. A god or even a demigod could handle what Dionysus offered easily, but a mortal? Not a chance. Dio smiled.

Eros held his hand out for a glass, and before he even saw him move, the glass was filled with beautiful, dark, red wine. "What are we toasting? Have the gods finally gotten you to behave?"

"Never! I'd rather be dead than listen to their rules! We're toasting love, immortality, and the hopefulness of soon being rather immoral as well!" Dionysus clinked glasses and made a pleasant face as he drank the entire glass.

Eros took a sip, and Dionysus put his hand on the bottom of the glass.

"Drink it up while it's chilled perfectly—or your mother will treat you like a baby again and start making you wear those loin rags once more. What a disgrace!"

That was all it took. Eros drained the full glass in a couple of swallows, wiped the drops from his chin and posed with his leg bent at an angle. He glared menacingly and shouted, "My mother has no more control over me than she has over you, Dio!"

Smiling his wide, drunken smile, he said, "You are so correct about that, Eros. You are so right about that." Dionysus filled another glass of wine.

They sat on the pedestal and drank the whole sleeve of wine.

Eros said, "This is the best wine you've ever made."

Dionysus laughed maniacally.

When Eros left his mother's garden, he was fairly tipsy. He had to be near Willow—no matter what. To his fuzzy brain, it was the only thing that made sense.

He found her alone in a hotel in some rat-hole, mid-American town. She was in bed. Eros had never glimpsed a more beautiful woman in his life. She was dressed in lingerie—or as close as he could imagine Willow wearing. She was a sight of utter perfection.

CHAPTER 29

You instill fear.
Should I be afraid?
It feels so right though.
Do I know you?
Do you know me?
But at night, I welcome you.
Take me in your arms.
Shelter me.

Looking down on Willow as she rested quietly, Eros was moved beyond words. Sliding into bed beside her, he gritted his teeth at the coarse sheets she was being forced to sleep on. From that moment forward, she would have the best of everything. Her body in tight lace and tiny underpants was enough to make him forget where he was. The blood began to rush to his loins. She was the most beautiful woman. She had the same long, straight hair as his beloved Psyche. They had the same cheekbones, and her full, red lips were made for kissing.

As he leaned in to kiss her lips, she moaned slightly. His manhood took a leap in his lap, and he crushed her lips to his, enfolding her small body. Another sleepy moan had him gasping for air and cursing his uncle for his wine. His mouth was so incredibly dry that he could barely swallow. Turning his back to his luscious Willow, he grabbed the glass of water that she kept on her bedside table, regardless of what hovel she was in. Gulping greedily, he drained the glass. He jumped up to refill it, and the world went dark.

Nothing was darker than Tartarus, the deepest underworld.

***

I awoke to sunlight spilling in through the crack in the curtains. *Why don't they make those things so they close completely?* I yawned and stretched, annoyed by how rough the sheets were against my skin and my dry mouth. I reached for her bedside glass of water.

It was gone!

I popped up like a jack-in-the-box. A man was on the floor of the small, shabby room. He was lodged between the bathroom door and the tiny space at the end of the bed. He looked dead, and a glass was still in his hand.

Did I kill him? "Oh my God! Eros? Please answer me!" I leaped out of the bed, yanked on sweatpants and T-shirt—as if it mattered—and rushed to his side. I was still groggy from the allergy pills. My hands shook badly, and I shook him gently. "Hello? Wake up! Is it you, Eros? Please? Please!" I screamed. When he didn't respond, I shook him again. "Eros!"

I shook with all my strength and even poured a cup of water over his head. Nothing. Finally, with all my might and a huge dose of adrenaline, I rolled him onto his back. I put my head on his sculpted chest to listen for a heartbeat, not a sound. *Why am I noticing his chest muscles while he is dying on the floor of a crappy motel in the middle of nowhere? Why did I give him those stupid pills?*

I opened my eyes and saw his chest rising gently. He was breathing! He was the most beautiful man I had ever laid eyes on, and my heart thumped heavily.

Flyn pounded on the door and called my name frantically. The door burst open, and Flyn took up the entire entry.

My eyes never left Eros's face. "What the hell have I done?" I screamed. "Oh my God, no, Eros, please, please, no!" I cried.

Flyn lifted me off the ground easily since my body was limp and lifeless.

I cried harder than I had ever cried. I was in shock as Flyn loaded me into the backseat of his car, belted me in, and drove off. I cried myself to sleep after hours and was cursed with no dreams. After two hours of restless sleep, I awoke again and cried for my dead love—my one and only Eros.

I wished I could simply die.

CHAPTER 30

I let Flyn drive, and I sobbed and slept. I felt sick and angry. I don't know how many hours passed or even days. Sometimes I was cold and in the dark or warmed by the sunlight, but it didn't matter. I don't remember eating or drinking or stopping to use the restroom. I was lost.

Flyn finally stopped at a small campground an hour from the commune and rented one of many cabins. If I had spoken a word to him since leaving Eros in that awful motel, I didn't remember it. My throat ached from crying and perhaps yelling. My eyes felt swollen and bruised, and I felt nothing inside but despair. I recalled some whispered words of regret from him and some gentle rubbing of my shoulders and neck.

As he lifted me out of his car to carry me inside to the couch, he kissed my temple softly. He went to grab a grocery bag that I didn't remember him buying. I didn't care what was in it, and I only wanted to melt again and look for Eros in my dreams.

Flyn went to the kitchen and began making lots of noise, unloading items, and moving pans and dishes. I couldn't fall back into my oblivion with all the noise. Just as I was about to scream at him to keep it quiet, my stomach rebelled.

I sat up so quickly that my head spun for a moment, and I must have made a sound. Flyn rushed into the tiny bedroom and fell to his knees in front of me. He held an ice-cold bottle of water out to me. His eyes looked like melted chocolate in the darkness of the cabin, and my heart lurched inside my ribs.

"Are you okay?" he whispered.

Nodding, I grabbed the water from him.

I drank half the bottle in one sip and immediately felt my eyes overflow as I was hydrated. My chin quivered, and I fought the aching in my chest.

Flyn wrapped his arms around me and pulled me onto his lap. My cheek pressed into his dirty shirt as he maneuvered us both onto the couch.

I couldn't speak.

Finally, Flyn sighed heavily and said, "We need to get to the bottom of this, Willow, so you can finally be happy. Let's get some food in you."

My stomach growled loudly.

He continued, "Then a shower, some clean clothes and a trip to see your parents."

All I could do was nod as he helped me off the couch and walked me to a small kitchenette with two barstools. As I eyed the stools, Flyn grabbed a chair from the office.

I gratefully—but not gracefully—sat down. I saw the bags he had brought in, and he began to cook almost every food item found in any convenience store in America.

He boiled water for macaroni and cheese with powdered cheese, opened a can of green beans and a can of pinto beans, and microwaved them together. He pulled out a can of tuna and three packets of mayonnaise. He met my gaze and raised his eyebrows in apology.

When my stomach voiced its hunger again, we laughed.

No! What am I doing laughing when my heart and world is broken?

Flyn grabbed my hands and held them between us, forcing me to look into his eyes. "I don't know what is going on here, but I'll help you find out. I only want you to be happy, and if I can't make you happy, then so be it." He shook his head and looked down at our feet. "I've never heard anyone cry for someone like that. If that's true love, then I hope he's alive and well."

I let the tears leak from my eyes and rested my forehead against Flyn's head. I clasped his hands tightly. "Me too, but I don't know. This is all so strange."

Standing up and moving away, he quickly made a plate and held it out. "First things first. You need to eat. Then shower!" he said, wiggling his nose.

I looked down at myself for the first time and noticed that my white T-shirt was mostly brown and gray. My sweatpants were stained with jelly.

"Here!" He handed me the plate. "You've lived off of jelly donuts for two days. You owe me for at least a dozen."

Turning around to make his own plate, I'm sure he missed my mouth tilting up into a tiny smile. I began to eat as if I had lived on jelly donuts for two days.

He handed me a soda. After I drank it, he handed me another. He ate his meal and tore into a bag of corn chips and the biggest bag of beef jerky I had ever seen.

With my stomach full and feeling safe in the company of such a sweet man, I drifted off to sleep as soon as my head hit the lumpy pillow. The bed dipped next to me, and I felt a whisper on my cheek.

"Sweet Willow, it is a difficult matter to keep love imprisoned. Don't give up, sweet girl. You will be together!"

And as quickly as it came, it was gone. I rolled on my side and went back to sleep. The next morning, the words haunted my waking hours in a way they never did during my sleeping ones.

CHAPTER 31

You belong to me.
No escape, no freedom
Follow my every word.
Slave, slave, slave.

Eros awoke with a massive headache in a cheap motel room in the middle of nowhere. He shook out the cobwebs, noticed the fallen glass, a pink sock, a blue ponytail holder, and some tinted lip balm beneath the bed. Reality dawned on him.

"Oh, Willow! No!" He dropped to the nasty carpet beneath him and repeated her name to Olympus and Tartarus. He was begging for help, and he knew his mother's allies would come to her aid. He needed some of her enemies on his side, and his first visit would be to Zeus. He would plead his case and explain his mother's vanity and betrayal. Zeus would understand. He had lived with the woman for millennia, after all, and she had tried to mess up her father's love life tool. He needed to see Zeus, but he had to see his awful mother first. He wanted to tear her apart. He would make her regret everything she had done to destroy his love. She would suffer if he had his way.

He needed to regroup, drink some ambrosia, and track down Willow. He assumed she would go directly to her parents' house, but Flyn was interfering. He didn't know how long he had been asleep or which way to look. He closed his eyes and took himself to the center of Hades. He went to the outer chamber of the goddess of the underworld, Persephone, a longtime rival of his mother's.

Black tapered candles floating in black candelabra greeted him. A voice as soft as a breeze said, "Follow me. She's been 'aspectin yous for a bitty time noe. Don't dawdle."

As the candles moved toward a set of massive black granite doors, he followed. He wondered if he had heard anything at all. He was familiar with the underworld and had visited several times, but he couldn't recall this particular spectacle. When they reached the double doors, he felt a brisk slap to his cheek.

The voice whispered, "That's for gawkin, you poor-mannered boy!"

It was dark.

He could hear the doors grinding open, and his shocked eyes began to see a flicker of firelight.

Grateful for any light and anxious to find Willow, he reached between the doors and tried to pull them open faster.

He felt a sharp pinch on his behind. "Don'ta be so rushing here. You aren't the first she asspectin' so don'ta get ahead a yourself or you be sorry!"

A strong tug on his ear had him moving back from the door.

"Ouch! Do you know who I am, you old bitty?"

"No, son, and I don'ta much care neither. I been waitin' at this door and carryin' them blasted candles for near a two century so don'ta be shoving at myself! It's my turn next."

Baffled, Eros looked toward the blank spot in front of him. The voice seemed to be located slightly below his ribs. "Do you mean you have to wait to have an audience with Persephone?"

"Agh! I don'ta know 'bout no audience with the spring queen, but I'm waitin' to see the dark princess. No, the missus is mournin' the loss of warmth. It's near wintry in some parts, lad."

"Where is she?" Eros practically jumped at the empty space in front of him.

"Well, well, temper there, son. She'll be in the gardens, of course. That way." A bright light flashed down a darkened hallway, stopping at a dark green door. It was the first color he had seen since arriving, and the light coming from under the door was yellow. It looked like heaven.

Grasping the door handle and preparing to enter, he had second thoughts. Persephone was usually depressed and angry when spring and summer ended, and she had to return to this dark place. *Perhaps I should proceed cautiously.*

Just as the thought crossed his mind, a lovely voice from the garden said, "Eros, darling boy, I've been expecting you. Come in. Come in and rest. Have some ambrosia, my dear."

At the word ambrosia, his mouth watered—and his knees felt weak. It had been a long day, and he needed to heal his body. He had no choice but to bow down to kiss the amulet Persephone wore to keep her down below for six months each year.

As he raised his head, a large goblet floated in the air. The scent of the nectar of the gods caused the blood to rush to his stomach, leaving his head light.

"Go ahead. No need for politeness. I can see your pain," Persephone cooed.

Eros grabbed the chalice and drained every drop.

CHAPTER 32

When we awoke, I was so disoriented that I almost confused the closet with the restroom, but Flyn guided me to the correct door.

I took a heavenly hot shower, brushed my teeth and hair, and put on the clean clothes that he had somehow purchased along our way. Emerging from the steamy, tiny room, I almost felt renewed until I remembered the words of my dream.

"You will be together." My step faltered, and my stomach took a chance to flip over. *Who is that voice? I know those words.*

Flyn looked disheveled on the unmade bed, and I felt guilty for all I had put him through in the past few days. I was so grateful he had come to bring me home that I almost threw my arms around him. When I noticed the strained look on his face, my eyebrows rose.

He grabbed his grocery bag of clothes and toiletries and passed me by like a breeze.

When I sat down to pull on the socks and shoes he'd purchased, the sun was in my eyes. I had slept for two days without noticing the scenery or passing time.

When the shower turned on, I glanced at the door. I needed fresh air and some breakfast for the two of us. It seemed only fair since Flyn had taken care of me during the drive home. I stepped out of the room to the smell of flowers and freshly cut grass, which was not a smell I would normally associate with a run-down campground. The smell of bacon lured me toward a small diner at the front entrance.

In the small, converted camper, fifteen retirees sat in groups of four or less around an old-fashioned bar with a few high-top tables scattered about an open space. I felt their eyes on me. I watched the floor closely to avoid conversation and planted myself on the first empty barstool I came to.

A menu miraculously appeared in front of me. I glanced up from under my wet hair—not knowing what to expect—and found someone in front of me who could have been my sister. She was blond, petite, and muscular. Her blue eyes stared through me. She smiled and said, "I'd go with the specials if I were you, but here's a menu anyway. Coffee?"

I could only stare and nod. I felt as if I were in a dream world.

Everyone returned to conversations I had so rudely interrupted by entering the place.

What in the world?

The young woman turned over my coffee mug, filled a to-go cup, and snapped a lid on top. "For your friend in the shower. Two specials for you?"

"Sure." I glanced down as the menu was swept away.

She swayed into the kitchen to turn in my order. She looked so familiar, but I was sure I had never seen her before. I watched beneath my drying bangs as she sashayed about, refilling coffee and water glasses and chatting amicably with the retirees.

I pressed my aching eyes into the palms of my hands for a good rub.

A chipper voice said, "Here ya go, sweetie. Two specials to go—and an extra little gift just for you. Don't open it until you get home because you'll need it then."

I looked up at her blankly, and she winked. "Be safe, Willow. Persephone is on your side."

Dumbfounded, I searched her face and landed on a nametag on her ample chest: *Seph*.

"What?" I asked dumbly.

"Go see your mother. She needs you." She turned her back on me and returned to the kitchen.

At the mention of my mother, I focused on my mission. I left a twenty-dollar bill on the bar and walked out. I had to find Flyn and get home as soon as possible.

CHAPTER 33

The commune seemed unusually brown and bleak for so early in the autumn. Everyone seemed to be inside, which was very strange. I was so worried about my mother and anxious to see her that perhaps I should have paid it more attention.

Flyn didn't mention it either.

As we pulled into the drive at my parents' house, I was struck by how much I had changed in the last weeks. I felt like years had passed.

Before Flyn could put the car in park, I launched myself out of the passenger side door. When I reached the front porch, I wrenched the door open so hard I flinched at the sound. As my eyes adjusted to the darkened room, I saw my father in a chair and my mother in a twin bed. He was erect and alert—but somehow smaller.

A shrunken version of Bren was holding his hand tightly. "Oh, Willow," she said breathlessly, as if I'd returned from a long walk.

I fell to my knees beside her bed. The surroundings blurred through my tears, and my heart pumped in my ears. "Oh, Bren! Please be okay! Mama! Please?"

She ran her fingers through my hair.

I gulped and spluttered in her lap, and she made soft cooing sounds, repeating my name.

I found my breath and raised my head to look at her. I knew she was sick, but this was too much to take in at once. Gone was her vivaciousness and life force, like a color disappearing from fabric after too many washes. Her hair had thinned and hung limply across the pillow. Her sunken cheeks and purple-circled eyes aged her beyond her years. She looked drained and small and sick.

My father looked toward the floor. He looked up and grabbed my knee.

I saw tears glide down his nose and said, "What in the world has happened? Have you seen the doctor? Been to the hospital? Dad?"

He was crying softly and looking down.

I turned desperately to search my mother's face for answers. She smiled weakly, and tears trembled on her lashes. "We are so happy to have you home, safe and sound!"

Gulping loudly, I cried harder into the blanket on her legs.

Please, help me. Help my family, I prayed. If anyone was listening, they didn't respond.

I must have fallen asleep at some point. I was cried out and exhausted from lack of food, sleep, water, comfort, and love. Life as I knew it was gone. My love's jealous mother had destroyed it. I couldn't stand it anymore. It had to end.

CHAPTER 34

I awoke to weak sunlight streaming through my window in my old room. It was either very early or very cloudy. Unsure of how I had gotten to bed and unaware of what I would face when I saw my mother again, I dressed frantically in the nearest clothes I could reach. I ran a washcloth over my face, quickly brushed my teeth, and rinsed my mouth.

I willed myself to head downstairs to check on Bren and forced my lungs to take a few long breaths. My mind didn't clear, but my hands shook a little less. *How could she have become so ill?* I had never seen my mother sick and was amazed that she had gone downhill so quickly. *What will I do if I lose her? Is such a thing even possible?* There were no orphans at the commune. They had simply moved in with family—born or chosen—and kept on living. The thought of losing my mother was unimaginable.

My father also looked sick, but I had chalked it up to exhaustion and grief. He had lost two daughters and their families. *What will I do if I lose my parents?* A few breaths later, I opened my door to the smell of breakfast and sickness. My stomach rumbled and revolted at the same time. I braced myself and headed downstairs.

My father was still slumped in a chair next to my mother's bedside. They seemed more tired and worn—if that was possible.

It dawned on my growling stomach that neither of them could possibly be creating the smells that were taunting me.

"Who's cooking breakfast?" I asked.

"That would be Seph, the nurse we hired to help us until Bren is back on her feet," my father mumbled.

Seph? I kneeled by my mother's bed and wrapping my hands around my parents' clasped hands. "What can I do for you? Can I help you while you rest? Where is everyone? And why aren't they helping you? You're obviously both sick, and I've never seen anything like this. I'm scared!" My lips began to quiver, and tears threatened to spill over.

Bren smiled serenely and beautifully. My mind melted into her soulful eyes. In my head, she said, "Do anything you can to defeat Aphrodite!"

I sat up straight, and startled my father with my abrupt move.

My mother smiled tiredly and whispered, "Go get something to eat, Willow. We need to talk."

"I'm fine," I said. *Not so fine—but I could be worse.*

"Go," she said. The strain in her voice forced me to move.

I pulled myself up to stand, and my legs quivered. My stomach growled loudly.

Bren patted my hand and said, "Go meet Seph. Get some breakfast—and then we can talk."

Reassured by her confidence, I turned toward the kitchen.

"I'd stick to the special if I was you, but make your choice. I cook what's available. Coffee, sweetie?"

My chin dropped to my chest. Seph smiled, and her eyes looked like cornflowers lit by a sunset.

I was mesmerized and speechless. "Don't I know you?" I reached for a chair and plopped down rudely.

"I noticed you haven't paid much attention to the gift I gave you at the diner. I thought we should discuss it. I left a note. Did you see it?"

"Note? Gift? At the diner? I'm so sorry! Was it pie? Or lunch? I'm sure it's ruined now, but—"

Seph fed me scrambled eggs, bacon, biscuits, and coffee. She told me an amazing tale about being a pawn in one of Aphrodite's love triangles. She claimed to know how to beat Aphrodite at her love game and said she could help free me from this terrible existence. The gift she had given me was to appease Aphrodite, but I was unsure exactly what that meant.

I was to deliver the box to the nearest makeup counter and not look inside for any reason.

I pondered her odd request and worried about my mother. I approached my parents sadly. They both looked so tired. I hiccupped back the sob in my throat, threatening to lose the best meal I'd had in days. I grasped Bren's hand.

Bren looked up at me through her lashes. "Go. Read. Your. Note," Bren said with complete seriousness.

Gulping a sob as tears ran down my face, I said, "Why? Why? Mama? Please help me!"

A smile spread across her face and she seemed to relax.

I felt my father's hand tense under ours.

She squeezed back, and without opening her eyes, she said, "Just don't look in the box, sweetheart. I love you so much! Go! Please."

I felt her hand relax and heard the snore she makes while she slept. Glancing quickly at my father's weary eyes, I dashed for my room and the package that might save the whole situation.

CHAPTER 35

I ran to my room and searched through my scrap pile of belongings. I found a perfectly white pie-shaped cardboard box. *How could I have forgotten this?* An envelope had my name scrawled across the front.

I pulled the tape from the envelope, and the smell of honeysuckle, wisteria, and freshly mowed grass wafted up to my nose. *Did this really come to me as a gift? In my rush to get home last night, did I forget it? After breakfast, I took it all to Flyn. Did he see it? Did he hide it from me? Would he do such a thing? It doesn't matter. If it helps my mother, anything is worth it. What else did Bren say?* "Don't look in the box!"

Is that it? I gently removed the envelope and peeled it open. On a piece of notebook paper, I saw a message. I had to blink before the words stood out.

Dear Willow,

I know what you're going through is pure torment, and I want to help you. To cut to the chase, you belong with Eros and only Eros. And don't shake your head at me!

I know you think you have it all figured out as most girls your age do. I remember, but this is different. You've been chosen. You won't understand immediately, but please do what I say. Take this box to the abandoned mall to the makeup counter and wait there. Inside the box, there is something Aphrodite can't resist. Don't look in the box— no matter how much you want to! Please! If you don't open the box, she will leave you alone. And you'll have the love you've always wanted.

Good luck,

Seph :))

The love I've always wanted? Belonging to each other? I feel as if I'm in another universe. How can my world flip upside down so quickly?

With my fists by my sides, I shouted, "Damn you, Eros! You night-stalking, son of a true purebred bitch! I'll break this spell, and you won't have anything to say about it! Leave me alone!" I was hyperventilating and tried desperately to calm myself down.

As my breathing slowed, my heart rate became steady. I grabbed up my duffel bag, stuffed the note and box inside, and headed to face my parents—and perhaps confront Seph about what she actually knew.

I ran downstairs, and the bottom floor was empty. I searched the kitchen and each room, but everyone had disappeared. I pressed my hand to my mother's bed. It was still warm. I threw my head back and roared.

Snatching my bag and pulling the keys from my pocket, I headed toward the mall.

This is done. Here and now!

***

I pulled into a parking space, quite crookedly, and left the car running. I barely remembered to put the car in park.

I rushed toward the entrance, but the doors were bolted. Huge chains and multiple locks barred my way. I ran to each entrance into the old building and felt my energy draining. All the doors were locked. *Can this be any harder? Hell, I don't even want Eros. I want my family to be left alone. I need my mother to be well. I have to break this curse.*

I headed back toward my car, and an automatic door opened, which startled me. Once my heart slowed, I could tell the door led into a massive department store. *This is it.* I walked in with my head held high, crossing into my destiny. I was ready for it to be over. I wanted to offer Aphrodite the one thing she couldn't resist, according to Seph. I just wanted it to be over and done with. I wanted my family whole and well again. I wanted my life to be my own again.

"I'm simply exhausted," I said to no one in particular. It became my mantra.

The store had closed several years earlier, and dust motes danced in the lazy sun that filtered through the dirty glass. I made my way past discarded boxes and displays to a faded and dark corner of the store that had once been a makeup counter. I could only hope I was in the right place. I put the package and note on the counter and sat on a cushioned chair that looked like it had been mauled by rats. I waited for my destiny to be determined so my mother could get well and my dreams could once again become my own.

Time seemed to slow to a crawl. I knew nothing would hurry the queen bitch. The darkness was suffocating even as the sun tried to break through. I shivered in the cold, insane spot.

I stretched my legs and felt intoxicatingly dizzy. The world around me melted away until it was simply the pie-shaped box full of something the bitch mother couldn't resist.

I can't say what made me reach for it—was it jealousy, rebellion, or closure? I have no idea. I snapped the box off the counter, threw the lid open, and stared.

The world faded to a dull, gray evening. I had no idea about the power. I let it flow through me until I collapsed. The world grew black. A woman laughed cruelly in the distance.

***

I dreamed in that black void of nothingness, and I remembered being told not to look in the box. Boredom and curiosity had once again overcome my willpower. *Lucky me!* I felt cold marble beneath my back and knew I was in a different time and place. My dream self sat up and saw a massive pile of grain.

"Divide these—and I may yet let you live!" a sharp voice yelled at me.

Shocked and dizzy, I couldn't find the voice. I returned my gaze to the pile in front of me. I realized that all sorts of grains were mixed together—and I didn't recognize all of them. It would be like counting grains of sand on the beach in a hurricane.

"Divide them! Now!"

I jumped at the fierceness in the voice. With trembling hands, I reached forward and began shifting the grains.

CHAPTER 36

"Willow? Willow, please wake up!" I heard it in the smallest place in my mind. It wasn't a full voice. It was an echo of a voice. "Willow!"

In the darkness, I felt pain in my ears. My head throbbed, but I was grateful to be warm. I pulled into the warmth, and my ears stopped ringing. The ache in my head became a nuisance instead of a pounding. I took in a deep breath to calm my heart, and ivy and roses filled my nose and my heart.

In shock, I willed my eyes to open. I forced myself to focus on the greenest eyes I had ever seen. They were the color of summer grass with a streak of gold around a black pupil. I needed to blink, but my eyes wouldn't close. Tears threatened to pour out of my eyes.

A gentle hand reached up and closed my eyes, but I could still see him. His eyes were glued to mine, and darkness overcame me again.

Eros wrapped me gently in a cashmere blanket on the softest bedding he could find. His lips barely brushed mine, and he breathed into the space between us.

"Willow." He exhaled his godly powers and his strength.

As our lips met, electricity sparked inside us both. I reached up and grasped him. Our bodies fit perfectly.

He lowered me back down onto the soft covers, and our eyes opened. There was no one else on the earth or in the universe but the two of us.

I said, "Oh gods, I love you! I'm sorry. I mean, you're beautiful and wonderful, and I love you!" *I couldn't speak a second ago—and now this?* I blinked, wrapped my arms around his waist, and whispered, "Eros, I love you so much. Don't let me down."

Darkness ascended on my world. Eros left me in the cashmere blanket, and I dreamed of life before this all happened. I dreamed about him.

***

Eros couldn't help Willow, but he knew someone who could defeat his mother's wicked plans.

Persephone, the goddess of spring, hated his mother as much as he did! He roared to the skies, "Seph, help her! Please?"

And she did.

CHAPTER 37

Why must our love be hidden?
Does our love hinder anyone?
Marriage, discrimination,
Hate, love, peace.
Live my life with you—
Until the end.

I gazed at the grains in front of me and desperately separated them, remembering my last dream.

Please help me! I continued working.

Hundreds of red-breasted robins flew down from the upper windows and began to separate the grains for me. I gasped and moved away. *How is this happening? Is it a dream? Am I that exhausted?*

It didn't matter. I fell asleep to the sound of beautiful spring robins and the smell of grass and dirt in the air. And I was grateful for it all.

Chapter 38

Eros stormed into the mountain palace. Mount Olympus had white columns, white granite, white rock, and white snow. It was a daunting place—a place of fear and extravagance. The gods and goddesses had other homes and temples, but Olympus was the best place to find them together.

Eros desperately needed them to agree unanimously—or as close as they could get—to his preposterous plan. He needed support against his mother. Since she had begun to ridicule Olympus and the power they wielded over the human world, he knew that most of her enemies would be there. It was his best chance.

With his bow across his arm and his quiver across his back, he nodded to Zeus, Hera, Persephone, Hades, and Neptune. As he crossed the floor, he made eye contact with his friends— Apollo, Jason (who owed him big time), and Adonis. His eyes pleaded with them to help him, and he fell to his knees in supplication to Zeus.

"Father, I beg you once again to lean toward my will. You know I have long since mourned the loss of my sweet Psyche, and I believe I have found her again in this world. Her name is Willow, and my mother is once again standing in the way of everlasting love. As the god of love, I ask you to look upon us in favor—regardless of what she says!"

Zeus grunted and turned in Hera's direction. "Don't look at me like that! You suck at love and fidelity, and so does Aphrodite. What the Hades should I say?"

Rolling his eyes at his wife, Zeus looked pointedly at Eros. "Son, what can I say? Your mother is the goddess of love, and you are merely her messenger. Perhaps I should call her here to ask her opinion?"

After a muffled gasp from Hera, Eros, and the rest of the assembly, Zeus looked up and asked, "What?"

Hera turned her steely eyes to him and muttered, "Humph!"

"Eros, what is it you wish for me to do in this situation? She's a mortal, and you're a god—you most choose. You can't have both."

EPILOGUE

I woke up in Eros's arms. I was groggy and had the driest mouth ever. I melted into his chest, and his heart beat in time with mine. I closed my eyes, drifted into his scent, and let out a long sigh.

"It's okay, baby. Sleep. I love you, Willow! It's going to be fine. Shhh."

He kissed her head and stroked her fine, straight hair. It felt like water under his fingers. Feeling her breath steadying and slow, he kissed her brow. "I'm here for you forever, sweetie," he whispered.

On the brink of dreaming, she whispered, "Yes. Forever, Eros. I love you too!" And she slept.

Poems

I see you there.
I look down on you, and I see you there.
So proud to see you laugh and smile,
It makes me happy to know you care
For people that I cared for there.
You may not see the blessing you are, to
people who need you, changed forever.
Your heart is strong, and your love is true, and
I want you to know that I'm proud of you.

--*-*-

Bright, exploding colors
Hurt the eyes and stimulate the mind.
Pseudomusic all around.
Speak in tongues.
Create odd things.
Calm and peaceful.
Blissful sleep.

-*-*-*-*

Red. The color of blood,
The flow of life.
Blue. The color of water,
The element of life.
Love. A necessity of life.

-*-*-*-*-

Oh, my muse,
You make me want to write songs
and poems about you.
You are my nutrition.
For without you, I am lost.
I am hungry. Please feed me.

-*-*-*-*-*

Invisible, silent—
Even when loud.
Nobody hears.
Nobody sees except to criticize.

-*-*-*-*-*

Cultures living within cultures.
People the country refuses to see.
Tribes dying.
"You can only live our way."

People vanish.
The only way they know how to
Communicate is thru wars,
Threats, poisons.
Who set these rules?
I will not live by them.
I will live by my own.
My rules have never killed,
Hurt, or threatened anyone.
Come live with me as once life was.

*_*_*_*_**

The sun god bathes upon your beauty.
He dashes across the skies in his
Golden chariot,
Gently hurling sunbeams for you to
Soak up.
Beams radiate miles ahead of you.
You have blinded everyone but me,
For I see the truth.

*_*_*_*_*_**

Rainbows pierce the waterfall.
Here wild birds and animals thrive.
Precious untouched soil,

Holder of many keys.
May an invisible gate hold you there
So no evil can touch you.
Eternal paradise.

-*-*-*-*-*-

Give to the gods.
Give to the goddesses.
May your fruit and seed be plentiful.
Rain makes rivers.
Play in the element of all being.

-*-*-*-*-

The Dionysian experience
Will expose an open path.
Ride the wave,
Drink of the sacred wine,
Dance to the flute,
Through the open window.
Don't ever let the window shut,
For if this happens, you will surely die.

-*-*-*-*

The yellow, pointed moon glows.
The wolves cry out your name.
Fairies run naked in the jaded forest,
Into a cave inside an ancient tree.

_--*-*-*-*-*_*

There they collect magic dust
And sing like the sirens in heaven.
When they are done, a frog carries them—
To the gentle and determined
ocean to collect light.
From there, they enter your dreams.
Sweet dreams.

About the Author

April Bonds grew up in northeast Texas in a happy, joyful home full of friends and family. A network of family and friends supported her. She enjoyed a childhood of laughter and graduated high school without knowing what to do. A lover of literature and words, she considered education, but she soon found her forte in the sciences.

After attending Texas A&M University, she graduated from the University of Houston with a BS in pharmacy. She owns a pharmacy that she runs with her husband and closest friends.

She resides near her hometown and family in East Texas. She writes poetry and teaches yoga in her spare time. Three beautiful children bless her home and keep her busy.

This is her first novel.